The Underground City

The Underground City

Anne Forbes

Kelpies

Kelpies is an imprint of Floris Books

This edition published in 2008 by Floris Books
© 2008 Anne Forbes

The publisher acknowledges a Lottery grant
from the Scottish Arts Council towards the
publication of this series.

British Library CIP Data available

ISBN 978-086315-637-3

Printed in Poland

For my daughter, Hanan,
with much love.

Contents

1. The Dare   9
2. Fire Damage   15
3. Mary King's Close   24
4. The Well at Al Antara   31
5. The Djinn   43
6. The Bank Robbers   51
7. Ali Baba   58
8. Ardray   64
9. Shades of the Past   73
10. Tracksuit and Trainers   81
11. Prince of Thieves   89
12. Police Probe   95
13. The Black Shadow   102
14. The Shadow Strikes Again   110
15. Lost in the Underground City   118
16. Chasing Shadows   127
17. Skating on Thin Ice   135
18. The MacArthurs' Return   144
19. Overture and Beginners   152
20. The Big Bang   158
21. The Lashkari Bazaar   164
22. The Hole in the Wall   171
23. Goblin Market   179
24. The Plague People   187

25. The Genie of the Lamp   194
26. Smoking Kills   201
27. An Uninvited Guest   209
28. Kalman's Revenge   215
29. Kabad to the Rescue   220
30. Nessie Flies the Flag   227
31. Showdown   231
32. Christmas Party   239
33. Christmas Presents   248
34. Wheel of Fortune   255
35. Star Suspects   263

1. The Dare

"I got Brian on his mobile," Jack Ellis said excitedly, putting down the phone. "He said he'd drive us out there this evening."

"Was he all right about it?" queried his friend Peter, doubtfully. Jack's brother was in the Sixth Form and had always been a bit of a stickler, so Peter found it hard to believe that he'd agreed to take part in their prank. But the fact remained that they couldn't go through with it unless *Brian* did the driving.

"He thought it was a great idea ... if we can persuade Lewis to go, that is," Jack assured him. "Said it was time somebody took him down a peg or two."

"Or even three," muttered Peter.

"Where is this village? What did you call it ... Al Antra?" asked Colin, whose father had only joined the oil company a few months previously.

"Al *Antara,* you mean?" Jack looked at him sharply. "Of course, I'd forgotten that you haven't been there yet. Come over to the window and I'll show you."

Colin looked out over a scene as far removed from Britain as you could imagine; for the bay window of the sparkling white villa overlooked a lush, green garden full of exotic plants and flowering bushes.

"Al Antara's a proper desert oasis," Jack said with a grin. "Rolling sand dunes, waving palm trees, an old stone well, the lot — definitely as seen in the movies! Look," he pointed, "over there, in the distance, at the foot of the Zor Hills. You can just see it. It's not really as far away as it looks."

Jack's house lay near the edge of the oil-company township and as Colin's eyes lifted to the barren reaches of desert that stretched beyond the garden, he picked out a ragged scatter of palms nestling amid sand dunes that rose in shades of brown and gold to the massive peaks of the Zor Hills.

"Got it," he nodded, again feeling very much the new kid on the block; for although it hadn't taken him long to find his way round the township, he knew he still had a lot to learn about the surrounding desert. Despite himself, he felt a growing sense of excitement. The set up here, he thought, was nothing *like* life back home but boy *was* he enjoying it!! School had turned out to be okay. He'd made friends with Peter and Jack right away and the only boy in the class that he hadn't much liked, a pillock called Lewis Grant, was due to leave the following day for Scotland.

"Is it tomorrow night he's going?" asked Colin, for Lewis's father had been posted to Aberdeen and their house was all packed up.

"Yeah, his dad's coming back from Bahrain tomorrow but tonight he'll be on his own in the house with only the house staff to look after him. Roger told me that he's really miffed that no one's throwing a farewell party for him. Believe me, he'll grab at the idea of spending the night at Al

Antara. He wants to go out with a bang and leave everybody talking about him, so he'll see this as his chance."

"And you can bet your bottom dollar he'll make sure that the story gets round before he goes! Lewis the brave! You just watch! He'll buy it!"

Colin looked concerned. "You mean he'll drive his dad's car out into the desert and sleep there?"

"Lewis has always done what he likes, when he likes!" grinned Peter. "And he'll be quite safe, you know. Nobody'll bother him out there. The bedouin won't go near the place after dark."

"You think he'll do it then?"

"Of course he will!" Jack said witheringly. *"Lewis Grant* refuse a dare! You must be joking!"

"Well, we'll soon know," announced Peter as a shining, silver 4x4 drew into the driveway. "Here he comes now ... and surprise, surprise ... he's driving himself!"

Lewis Grant winced as the full force of the desert heat hit him as he jumped down from the cool interior of the jeep. Slamming the door shut, as though he drove his father's car every day of the week, he waved casually to the group of boys clustered in the bay window of the flat-roofed, white villa. Pleased that there was an audience to witness his arrival, he flicked back his long, black hair and swaggered up to the front door.

"Hi, there," he said, walking through to the living room and throwing himself into an armchair. "Is there anything to drink, Peter? I'm gasping!"

"Sure, hang on. We've bags of cola in the fridge."

"How come you're driving your dad's car, Lewis? Does he know?" Jack asked breathlessly.

"Don't be daft, Jack! Of course he doesn't *know*. He's in Bahrain just now. One of the BAPCO wells is on fire and they're getting Boots & Coots in."

The mention of the famous firefighters impressed the boys and Lewis preened himself; being the son of the Managing Director of one of the biggest oil companies in the area certainly had its advantages.

"But taking the 4x4 ..."

Lewis sat up. "What on earth did you expect me to do?" he demanded. "You didn't really think I was going to leg it all the way over here in this heat, did you? It's fifty degrees out there, in case you hadn't noticed!"

"Didn't the house staff try to stop you? I mean, your mum's in Edinburgh, isn't she? They're responsible for you."

"Yeah! So responsible that they're all going to some dance at the club tonight! Anyway, it'd take more than the staff to stop *me!* They know that Dad has been letting me drive on the private roads for ages and anyway, I'm so good now that I could pass my test tomorrow if I wanted." He shrugged at their doubtful expressions. "Forget it, for Pete's sake! What have you all been up to?"

"Not a lot. Reading comics mostly," Jack said. "My dad bought a pile from the bookshop in the souk. This one's really good," he chucked it over to him. "It's all about djinns."

"Djinns?" queried Lewis, leafing through the pages.

"Yeah, you know ... desert spirits ..."

"I wonder if it's really true," Peter said dreamily. "There's one about a man who goes into a ruined city in the desert that's supposed to be haunted ..."

"And he sees djinns?" mocked Lewis. "Don't be so gullible!"

"*I* think it's true, Lewis. I don't care what you say," Jack said, his eyes gleaming. "*I* think there *are* djinns. It says they live in trees and houses and old wells ..."

"There could be some in that old ruined village near the hills," agreed Peter in a voice that was carefully casual. "My dad says the Arabs won't live in it 'cause they're scared of ghosts. And djinns *are* ghosts, aren't they?"

"You mean at whatsit ... Al Antara? Rubbish!" Lewis said dismissively. "We've been to Al Antara dozens of times and we've never seen anything or anybody. The whole place has been crumbling to bits for years."

"We've never been there at night, though. Maybe that's when they come out," Jack said, sitting up suddenly.

"Hey, that's an idea!" Peter interrupted, his eyes shining. "I'd love to go there at night! Just think what it'd be like to see a djinn!"

Lewis's eyebrows lifted in disbelief. "You?" he sneered, "at Al Antara in the middle of the night? Don't give me that, Peter!" He leant forward and flicked him with the pages of the comic. "You'd be scared stiff!"

Peter looked suddenly furious. "Well, if *you're* so brave," he snapped, "why don't *you* go and spend the night there! Go on, Lewis! I dare you!"

2. Fire Damage

When five magic carpets sailed over Edinburgh, Scotland's elegant capital, and landed in the garden of a small house in Holyrood Park, close to the towering hill known as Arthur's Seat, they didn't cause the kind of sensation you might expect — the simple reason being that as they were magic carpets, nobody could actually see them as they flew over the city.

It was only when their riders stepped onto the garden path of the little cottage that they became visible and if, by any chance, you have visions of star-studded wizards and magicians appearing out of the blue, then I'm afraid I must disappoint you. The MacLeans are a fairly ordinary family; probably the last people in the world you'd have expected to possess magic carpets and even Sir James, a Member of the Scottish Parliament and the owner of a very successful distillery, is not your average magic carpet traveller. Having said that, mind you, they're not all that ordinary really as Kitor, the large, black crow perched on Clara MacLean's shoulder, can talk.

The crow flapped into the air as Clara got off her carpet and she watched with a smile as he headed for the slopes of Arthur's Seat. Kitor had been grumbling about his empty belly more or less all the way from Jarishan and hopefully, she thought, it wouldn't be too long before he found some supper.

If not … well, the freezer was full and she could always defrost some chicken livers for him.

Travelling backwards and forwards over Scotland by magic carpet was nothing new to any of them and Clara's father, John MacLean, one of the Park Rangers on Arthur's Seat, merely turned round casually to check that they'd all arrived safely before moving towards the house, fishing in his pocket for his keys. His son, Neil, a tall, dark-haired lad, looked doubtfully at the five carpets that hovered round him at knee level. "We don't need the carpets any more, do we, Dad?" he queried. "Shall I send them back to the hill?"

Instinctively, they all turned to glance up at the looming bulk of Arthur's Seat, the hill in the middle of Edinburgh that looks for all the world like a sleeping dragon. Over the years, the MacLeans had learned many of its secrets, including the fact that the interior of Arthur's Seat was home to the MacArthurs, a little people — you can call them faeries if you like — whose adventures had, on several occasions, involved them in the affairs of witches, magicians, dragons and goblins.

"Yes, do that, Neil," nodded his father as he turned the key in the lock. "Send them back and mind and say thank you!" He pushed the door open against the pile of post and newspapers that had collected in the few days of their absence. "Sir James won't need his carpet again, either," he added. "He left his car here, remember?"

His wife turned to the tall, elegantly-dressed man who was trying vainly to smooth creases from the trousers of his best suit. Although he enjoyed flying on magic carpets, they had, Sir James reflected, their disadvantages and being open to the elements was one of them. It had been a long flight from Lord Rothlan's estate at Jarishan and he felt sadly crumpled and in need of a hot bath.

"I love flying on the carpets," he muttered, "but there's a lot to be said for using magic mirrors. It's quicker for a start and you don't get blown to pieces."

"Look on the bright side, Sir James," Neil said, watching the magic carpets become invisible again as they soared over the garden wall towards the green slopes of the hill. "At least it didn't rain!"

"You'll come in and have a cup of tea before you go home, won't you, James?" Janet MacLean offered, untying the scarf that she'd wound round her dark hair. "We all need something warm inside us."

"Yes, do have some tea with us, Sir James!" urged Clara. "We've got so much to talk about! It *was* a fabulous wedding, wasn't it?"

They wandered into the kitchen where Mrs MacLean, still in her coat, filled the kettle.

"Didn't Lady Ellan look beautiful? She made a lovely bride," her mother remarked, taking mugs out of the cupboard. "And Lord Rothlan is *so* handsome. Really, I felt quite tearful."

"Well, they'll be in their new palace in Turkey by this time," the Ranger said.

Mrs MacLean smiled a trifle ruefully. "I wouldn't have minded a palace as one of *my* wedding presents," she said. "The Sultan's very generous, isn't he?"

"He's been generous to us all, one way or another," smiled Sir James. "Think of the presents he's given us and the lovely holidays we've had in Turkey."

"And I wouldn't worry too much about not having a palace, Mum," grinned Clara. "Just imagine how long it would take to clean a hundred rooms!"

"It's a pity we couldn't have gone with the MacArthurs, though," Neil muttered enviously. "They'll be having a fabulous time at the Sultan's palace."

"Yes, but we could hardly have gone with them, Neil," his mother said reasonably. "Your dad has his work to see to and your half-term holiday is over already. You'll be back at school tomorrow."

"The Sultan will invite us again, Neil, don't worry," his father said. "He'll always be grateful to us for getting his crown back."

"Your dad has a point," smiled Sir James, picking some newspapers out of the pile of junk mail that the Ranger had brought in. He flicked idly through the headlines and then stiffened in horror. "Good heavens!" he gasped, "there's been a fire at The Kings!"

They looked at him in alarm as he unfolded *The Scotsman* and showed them the headlines. "A fire!" said Neil in horror. "At The King's Theatre?"

"James! Your pantomime! What on earth will you do?" asked Mrs MacLean, looking distressed.

"When did it happen?" Clara asked. "The theatre didn't burn down completely, did it?"

Sir James shook his head as he scanned the report. "It happened ..." he looked at the date on the paper, "it must have happened the day before yesterday. It hasn't burned down but there was a lot of damage inside ... mainly to the stage!" He lowered the paper and looked at them seriously. "If what this says is true then it looks as though *Ali Baba* might not come off after all. It'll be a real blow to Children's Aid if we have to cancel it!"

"Sir James, you *can't* cancel it!" cried Clara. "I mean ... what about Matt Lafferty?"

They all looked at one another in dismay — for persuading Matt Lafferty to star in *Ali Baba and the Forty Thieves* had been a stroke of genius on Sir James's part. Lafferty's meteoric rise to fame was the ultimate success story as the comedian, after winning a TV talent show, had become famous overnight. He was funny, fabulous and totally fantastic. Neil's heart sank at the thought that *Ali Baba* might not happen, for Lafferty's personality had transformed the show.

Clara's words echoed his mood. "I couldn't *bear* it if it had to be cancelled," she said, looking distraught. "We're having so much fun, aren't we, Neil?"

Neil nodded. When rehearsals had started, Sir James had sensed their enthusiasm for the pantomime and his offer to have them included as extras in the crowd scenes had been met with rapturous excitement. The theatre, Neil had decided, was totally brilliant and he'd certainly never thought, when he'd voted for Matt in the TV Show, that he'd find himself acting on stage beside him.

"Matt Lafferty's absolutely magic as the Grand Vizier!" Clara continued earnestly, looking pleadingly at Sir James. "The rehearsals are a laugh from start to finish. You just *can't* cancel it, Sir James!"

Sir James smiled and ruffled her hair. "I'll do my best," he assured her but his face was serious as, taking his car keys from his pocket, he turned apologetically to Mrs MacLean. "I won't have that cup of tea after all, Janet," he said. "I'd better get home at once. Lots of people must have been trying to get in touch with me."

"I'm sure they have," nodded the Ranger as he followed him to the door. "Let us know what happens."

Sir James smiled wryly at Clara as she held the front door open for him. "Don't worry about it too much, Clara," he smiled. "All is not lost! We might be able to put *Ali Baba* on at another theatre, you never know!"

"That'd be fab," she said, her expression lightening at the thought. "I'll keep my fingers crossed!" And they waved as Sir James reversed his car out of the driveway and drove off.

"Well, of all the things to happen," Mrs MacLean said. "What else does it say in the papers, John?"

"*The Evening News* says much the same as *The Scotsman*. It happened on Friday night ... an electrical fault ... no suspicious circumstances."

"Oh, Dad! I hope Sir James finds somewhere else to put it on. We love being in it even though we only have bit parts."

"It was good of him to arrange that," Janet

MacLean nodded, "but don't build your hopes up too much. It'll be quite difficult to find another theatre, you know. Places like The Lyceum, The Festival Theatre and The Playhouse all have their own shows planned for Christmas and the New Year. I can't think where he could hold it. It's a big production and, quite frankly, you can't put stars like Matt Lafferty in a small hall."

Neil and Clara sat in subdued silence round the fire that evening. Mrs MacGregor, the school janitor's wife, who had been looking after Mischief for the weekend, had brought her back and the little cat, glad to be home, was stretched out blissfully on the hearth.

"If she gets any closer, I'm sure her fur will singe," Neil grinned, looking up from a book.

Mischief opened one eye and looked at him before shutting it again and stretching herself lazily.

"I swear that cat understands everything we say," mused Neil.

A scrabbling noise made them turn and Clara got to her feet as Kitor nudged his ungainly way through the cat flap in the window and fluttered towards her.

"Kitor," she cried as he landed on her shoulder. "I wondered where you'd got to!"

"I thought I'd just give the hill the once over in case there was anything your dad should know about. Especially while the MacArthurs are in Turkey," croaked the crow, settling his wings and cocking a wary eye at Mischief who sat up, looked at him balefully through slitted, green eyes, and started to clean herself minutely.

Although they had tried, neither Neil nor Clara had ever been able to work out how they managed to understand Kitor, for he certainly wasn't speaking English as such. Somehow his croaks and caws formed words that they could hear in their heads but the sound, as Clara pointed out, didn't seem to come through their ears.

"School again tomorrow?" croaked Kitor, his bright, black eyes looking at the scatter of exercise books on the table.

"Only in the morning," Neil said. "I've got a school trip in the afternoon."

"So you have," said Clara, looking up. "Mary King's Close! I'd forgotten about that!"

"Mary King's Close?" queried the crow. "Does it still exist?"

"It's buried underneath the High Street," Neil explained to the crow. "When the plague came to Edinburgh a lot of the old town was sealed off and new houses were built on top of the old ones. Miss Mackenzie was telling us that there's a real network of old streets and alleyways under Edinburgh."

"An Underground City," Clara breathed. "It'd be great to explore it."

"I don't know about that," frowned her brother. "Graham Flint said that there are closed cellars down there that still have skeletons in them and the Council won't open them up in case the plague gets out and infects people."

Clara frowned doubtfully. "Trust Graham to come up with something like that," she said. "It *is* supposed to be haunted, though, isn't it? The newspapers were full of it when the Close first opened. Lots of people said they were pushed by invisible hands!"

"I'd forgotten that," said Neil, sitting up straight, his brown eyes gleaming with excitement. "I think I'll wear my firestone tomorrow! Then, if there *are* any ghosts, I might be able to see them!"

Kitor shifted uncomfortably on his claws. "I wouldn't if I were you," the crow said seriously. "Ghosts and magic don't really mix. Ghosts are spirits of the dead, you know; they're not magic people like the MacArthurs and they could harm you."

Clara looked at Kitor doubtfully but, even as she did so, she knew that Neil wouldn't take the crow's advice. The thought of being able to see ghosts had brought a sparkle to his eyes and although he laughed and said he didn't believe in them, she was quite sure that he would wear his firestone to school the next day.

3. Mary King's Close

"I tell you, he can see us," Mary King snapped in exasperation. "His eyes have been following us around ever since he came into the Close."

The ghosts eyed one another uncertainly. "But, Mistress King, how can he see us? He's just a boy and he's human. How can *he* see us when the others can't?"

"How should I know?" Mary King replied. "I only know that he can."

"Could he help us sort out the *other* lot, do you think?" muttered a ghost, known to all and sundry as "the old Codger."

"You mean Murdo and Wullie?" Mary King looked serious as she turned her mind to this other, more pressing, problem.

"Well," the old Codger pointed out reasonably. "We've tried everything in our power to get rid of them, haven't we? Pushing them around, freezing them solid, the lot ... and nothing's made any difference. They still come back every night."

A pretty, young ghost twirled a lock of hair around her long fingers. "At least this boy might be able to talk to them," she pointed out.

"Clarinda's right," agreed Mr Rafferty, a tall ghost who sported a curly white wig and a suit of elegant gold brocade. "I think we should ask him if he can do anything. Murdo and Wullie are getting just a wee bit too close to the Plague People for my liking!"

This produced a fearful silence as they looked at one another in horror, for the Plague People were something else. Each and every ghost knew that should the drifting, boil-encrusted horrors escape from their sealed prisons in the Underground City, they would not only infect the people of Edinburgh with the Black Death but they themselves would be affected and fade away completely. The ghosts, shuddering at the thought of losing what was left of their substance, turned questioningly to Mary King.

"As you say, Mr. Rafferty, they *are* getting too close," she said, pondering the matter. "I suppose we could talk to this boy. At least it's worth a try!"

And with that, all the ghosts turned and looked at Neil speculatively.

Neil looked back at them and shivered. He had seen their lips moving and although he was too far away to hear what they were saying, he could guess that they were talking about him. They must have realized that he could see them. He swallowed hard. Maybe it hadn't been such a good idea after all to wear his firestone, for from the moment he'd stepped into Mary King's Close, he had been able to see the ghosts perfectly and they scared the living daylights out of him. He hadn't really given much thought to what it would be like to see a ghost, nor had he had any concrete idea of what a ghost might actually look like. He'd supposed, again vaguely, that perhaps they'd be the sort of drifting white shapes he'd seen in films but the reality took his breath away. They were awful.

"Boooo!" Neil's heart pounded and he gave the most enormous start.

"Scared of ghosties, Neil!" crowed Graham Flint as his mates burst out laughing.

Miss Mackenzie turned and at the sight of Neil's white face, beckoned to Graham who sauntered idly up to her.

"Do you wish to stay here and take the tour with the rest of the class, Graham?" she asked.

"Yes, please, Miss."

"Then we'll have no more ... silly behaviour," she said sternly. "Honestly," she said to the tour guide, who had introduced himself as Stan, "I sometimes despair of this class!"

Stan, dressed for the part in a black velvet coat, knee breeches, a ruffled shirt and buckled shoes, had already raised covert giggles and sly nudges from Graham Flint's little gang and was on the alert for trouble. On the plump side, he had an engaging grin and looked kindly at Neil. "They all try it on," he said, comfortingly. "Don't let it worry you, laddie. If there are any ghosts here I'll eat my hat, I promise you!"

Two or three ghosts, who had been hovering angrily around Graham Flint, creased up at this remark and Neil gave a sickly smile. It was just as well, he reckoned, that Stan wasn't wearing a hat.

"You're not looking very well, Neil," Miss Mackenzie frowned, looking at him searchingly. "You can wait upstairs if you want. It's really quite airless down here," she added with a shiver. "To tell you the truth I feel a bit strange myself."

As two perfectly horrible ghosts were standing at her elbow, Neil wasn't at all surprised that she felt a bit strange. They looked reasonably solid for ghosts but as they had just drifted through a brick wall he knew they were, as Kitor had said, spirits of the dead. The two men were dressed like Stan, in old-fashioned coats and breeches, but many of the others that were drifting in and out wore rags fit only for scarecrows. There were women, too, he noticed. Some were quite respectably dressed but many were thin hags that hugged tattered shawls round their skinny frames, their faces drawn and grey. It was their eyes that frightened Neil the most, however, for they weren't proper eyes but black holes that had no depth.

Neil gulped and shook his head. "I'll be all right, Miss Mackenzie," he assured her.

Stan gathered them together and led them through a passage into the next house. As they followed him, Neil was glad that Miss Mackenzie had stayed beside him for there seemed to be more ghosts than ever drifting round the rooms and just as he was quite sure that they had come to see what he looked like, he also knew that he was the only one who could see them.

The first indication Neil had that the ghosts were on his side was when a hefty ghost gave Graham Flint an equally hefty push that knocked him into a wall.

"Who did that?" he yelled. "Miss Mackenzie! Somebody pushed me!"

Miss Mackenzie looked round. "But Graham,"

she said, "the only people near you are your … er … best friends …"

This was very obviously true, even to Graham. He glowered at them accusingly. "Which one of you was it?" he demanded furiously.

"It wasn't me!" they all chorused together.

Miss Mackenzie's lips twisted as she hid a smile. "The standard response!" she said to Stan, who was standing beside her, looking puzzled. Now Stan, who had in his time, taken many school groups round the Close, had immediately written Graham down as a troublemaker and had been keeping a wary eye on him in case he tried to nick any of the exhibits. It so happened that he had been looking in Graham's direction when he had thumped against the wall and was quite ready to swear that nobody *had* pushed him.

Nerves tingling and senses suddenly alert, Stan continued taking them round but it wasn't long before he realized that this tour was definitely something else. There was nothing he could put his finger on, for the kids looked perfectly normal and attentive; he just knew within himself that something weird was going on. He looked round apprehensively, visited by the oddest notion that somehow they'd travelled back in time; even the set displays seemed to owe more to the seventeenth century than the present day.

By this time, Neil had discovered that the ghosts were cold. He'd noticed it when he'd walked through one by mistake and then felt a fool as he'd muttered "sorry." Although he was quite sure that no one else could see them, there was no doubt, he thought, that they were affecting the atmosphere of the place. Stan was no longer as bright and cheery as he had been when they'd started and without being consciously aware of it, the class had drawn together in a tight-knit group as though they could sense the spirits drifting around them.

Neil saw to his amusement that six burly ghosts were standing firmly round Graham Flint who looked as though he was about to freeze solid. His face was white with cold, the tip of his nose shone red and his eyes were desperate. Then the unthinkable happened. Graham Flint — the tough guy, the bully of the school for as long as Neil could remember — Graham Flint began to cry.

Miss Mackenzie looked flabbergasted, as well she might. Neil hid a grin and the rest of the class looked alarmed and excited at the same time. We'll be texting one another about this all evening, thought Neil.

"It *is* cold, isn't it!" Stan tried to make light of the wrenching sobs that emanated from Graham in heaving, hiccupping snorts. "No central heating in those days, I'm afraid," he announced, rubbing his hands together and deciding there and then to cut the tour short. "Now, we'll just go through this door here and you'll be in Mary King's Close itself."

Neil gasped as he stepped into the gloomy, lamp-lit close that curved steeply downhill. A vague mist curled eerily round the houses and the atmosphere was strange, heavy and oppressive. The ghosts were there, too; some clustered in the doorways of the narrow, cobbled alley while others peered at him through the barred windows on either side of the close. He shivered as the grim reality of the seventeenth century curled about him; for although picturesque, it was an old, old street that spoke of grinding poverty and deprivation. It petered off into distant darkness and, looking up between the high walls, Neil saw that there was no strip of sky to lighten the gloom; just the dark outline of beams and stones.

"Those are the foundations of the City Chambers," Stan said quietly, thankful that the tour was over at last. "They didn't bother to demolish the old city in these days. They just built right over it."

It was time to go. Miss Mackenzie fussed around counting them all. Never, she thought, had a class formed a neater, straighter line faster than this one. They all looked cold, pinched and, like herself, desperately anxious to leave. Neil stood beside Stan at the end of the line and was just about to move off when he saw the writing on the wall and froze as he read what it said.

"Come on, laddie. It's time to go," Stan gestured encouragingly as the rest of the class moved off.

Neil didn't hear him. He stood rooted to the ground for, written in huge letters in a blood-red, glowing script that covered the walls of the houses, was a message. A message for him.

Neil. Come again. We need your help.

Mary King.

4. The Well at Al Antara

Lewis Grant bumped over the sand track in the 4x4 feeling excited and, if the truth be told, more than a little scared. Despite his boasts, he wasn't nearly as confident about driving on his own as he'd let on to Peter and the gang. So far, however, all had gone well. He'd often been to Al Antara in the past and he more or less knew the route — anyhow, there was no way he was going to get lost.

Nevertheless, as the track wound its way steadily across stretches of open desert, he started to worry for it was turning out to be a much longer journey than he'd remembered. But then, he supposed, when they'd been on desert picnics, he'd always been with friends; talking all the way without really looking at the scenery.

He drove on, clutching the steering wheel tightly and wishing that he'd never agreed to the ridiculous dare but when he topped a rise and saw before him the long, low, black tents of a bedouin encampment, he triumphantly punched the air with both hands; for beyond it he glimpsed the palm trees that marked the oasis of Al Antara.

He'd forgotten about the Arabs but wasn't particularly bothered about them as he knew they never went near the village at night. Most of them worked for the oil company anyway. Nevertheless, he took care to bypass the tents at a distance so that no one would see that it wasn't a man in the

driving seat. The bedouin, however, are noted for
their razor-sharp eyesight and as the sheikh of the
tribe watched the vehicle bump its way towards
Al Antara, he looked thoughtful. The driver was a
boy — in itself disturbing — and he was heading
for the oasis.

"Ya, Hassan," he beckoned to one of his sons.
"Take the pick-up and go to the office of Mr
Williams. Tell him that this vehicle ..." he wrote
the number on a piece of paper and handed it to
him, "this vehicle, driven by a boy, is heading for
Al Antara. He is on his own and I am worried for
him. It'll start to get dark soon ..."

Hassan's face suddenly changed to one of alarm.
"Father, look! A *shimaal!*" He pointed a quivering
finger in the direction of the distant township.

Sheikh Rashid swung round and let out a yell
that echoed round the tents.

"Shimaal! Shimaal!" His words rang round
the camp. Sand was hastily thrown over the fires
and children, animals and anything moveable was
grabbed and thrust into the relative safety of the
tents as the sandstorm swept down on them, the
billowing clouds of dust and grit shutting out the
sunlight as it rolled in a furious, swirling mass
across the desert, carrying everything before it.

Lewis drove on towards Al Antara and so anxious
was he to get there before darkness fell that he
forgot to look in his rear-view mirror, thus missing
the dreadful sight of the approaching storm billowing in behind him. The first hint that something
was wrong was when the palm trees at Al Antara

disappeared. He blinked. It was impossible. They had been there, just a few hundred yards away, as clear as crystal, and now they had gone. Then a burst of wind hit the car and within seconds the vehicle was surrounded by whirling clouds of sand that quite successfully blotted out both desert and sky and reduced his world to the inside of the 4x4. Driving was impossible. He put on the brakes hastily and switched off the engine. Now what was he going to do?

The *shimaal* hit the oil-company township just as Brian was preparing to take the boys to Al Antara. He grinned at them as they loaded their gear into the jeep and hid a smile at the stuff they'd brought. He actually had no intention of letting Lewis stay in Al Antara all night and once the boys had had their joke, he'd get Lewis to follow him back to the township. But if they really thought they were going to scare him with their collection of Halloween masks and ghost costumes, they were, he reckoned, doomed to disappointment. Stuff like that wouldn't faze Lewis for a minute.

At that moment, a strong gust of wind swept through the garden, bending the palm trees and blasting them with a wave of choking, dusty grit.

Colin grabbed at Peter in an effort to stay on his feet. "What's happening?" he gasped, hardly able to see as the sand got into his eyes and up his nose.

"It's a sandstorm," gasped Peter. "A *shimaal.*"

"Quick, everyone," Brian snapped. "Back into the house. There's no way we can travel in this!"

Once inside, they watched from the window as the *shimaal* howled and screamed round the house like a banshee with whooping cough. Brian looked worried and reached for the phone. His mother and father were visiting friends but he knew he had to tell them what had happened so that the company could send out rescue teams. His heart sank. What they were going to say when he told them that Lewis Grant, of all people, was stuck out in the desert in the middle of a *shimaal,* he didn't know — but he could guess.

"Do you think Lewis got to the oasis?" queried Peter half an hour later, as Brian looked at his watch yet again.

"He should have," was the answer. "If he didn't, then I only hope he'll have had the sense to obey the first rule of the desert."

"What's that?"

"Never get out of your car in a sandstorm."

To be fair, it actually wasn't Lewis's fault that he left the car. As he'd brought a bottle of water and a six-pack of soft drinks with him plus a powerful torch and a good supply of comics to while away the hours until daylight, he'd settled down in the car quite happily at first, although it was definitely eerie with the wind and sand howling round outside. Without air conditioning, however, the inside of the car gradually became more and more uncomfortable. A fine dust laced the air and he shifted restlessly as it got hotter and hotter and as his throat dried up, gulped down more and more of the soft drinks until he saw, with a prickle of worry, that there were very few cans left. Not being able to see anything was scary as well. He tried hard to concentrate on the adventures of his hero, Superman, but every so often he lifted his eyes and frowned worriedly as gusts of wind rocked the car until he really thought that it might topple over.

A normal sandstorm might, indeed, have rocked the car a little but Lewis didn't know that this was no ordinary sandstorm. The bedouin didn't go to Al Antara after dark because they knew there was a djinn there and that it came out at night. It was not just superstition. They knew! From time to time, Mr Williams from the oil company tried to persuade them to return, rebuild the houses and make the oasis their home but they were always steadfast in their refusal. Mr Williams could say what he liked, but a djinn was, after all, a djinn.

As the 4x4 gave a particularly violent lurch, Lewis grabbed at the door for support. His hand hit the door handle and in a triumphant roar of wind and sand, he tumbled out into the storm. The door then slammed shut as the vehicle righted itself. Crying with frustration he tried to open it, and couldn't. It must have stuck! Pulling his T-shirt over his mouth to keep out the sand, he felt his way round to the passenger door, tripping over his torch as he did so. He sighed with relief as he picked it up and stuffed it into his pocket. It would be getting dark soon and he'd need the light. Again he struggled to open the doors. He knew perfectly well that he hadn't locked either of them but despite his frantic efforts, neither would budge. There was only one thing for it. He'd have to take shelter in one of the houses at the oasis for no one could survive for long in the suffocating air of such a storm.

Although Lewis didn't have far to walk, the heat, the wind and the stinging sand scoured him like sandpaper. Desperately he stumbled on, quite unable to believe that this was actually happening to him. He managed to stiffen his resolve for a while by pretending that he was one of the heroes in his comic books but fear overtook him when he realized he was nearly exhausted and wouldn't be able to go much further.

It was then that the old, worn stones of the huge well at Al Antara loomed before him and he sobbed with relief as his hands clutched thankfully at its rim. Water! He could smell it and was so thirsty that he could think of nothing else.

The water in the well was sweet, he knew, for the Arabs had offered him some to drink when he'd visited the oasis with his parents, a while back. It had been cold and delicious, and his mouth was so dry that he could hardly wait to taste it again. Confidently, he looked up through the gloom to the rickety, pulley-like affair that held the bucket and bit his lip in dismay as, amid the swirling sand of the storm, he saw a tangle of wreckage that sprawled crazily over one side of the well. It had been blown down by the force of the wind and although he grasped one of the wooden supports and tried to lift it, he found it surprisingly heavy. Even if I could manage to pull it up, he thought despairingly, the storm would probably just blow it over again.

There was, however, another way to get to the

water; a more dangerous way. He looked over the edge of the well and there it was — a flight of stone steps that curved down its inner wall into the gloom. His parents, of course, had not allowed him to climb down the well but he'd often watched the Arabs clambering up and down if the bucket had stuck or the ropes got tangled. He didn't give himself time to think. He knew he had to get down to the water, for never before had he had such a raging thirst. Swiftly, he swung his leg over the top and balanced himself shakily on the first of the steps that curved down in a gentle spiral towards the water. He knew he had to be quick. Daylight was starting to fade and in the desert, darkness falls swiftly.

He took the torch from his pocket and flicked the light on the worn steps that jutted out from the wall. Fortunately, the well was wide and the steps broad enough to give him a welcome sense of security. Thank goodness his mother couldn't see him now, he thought, as he started downwards. She'd totally freak!

Despite the desert heat, the air in the well was cool and moist. He breathed it in gratefully as he followed the staircase down, but as he went further and further into the depths, the walls seemed to close in on him and at one stage he wondered if he'd ever reach the bottom. The torchlight, however, gave him confidence and eventually he reached the last step where a wide ledge gave onto a pool of dark water that lapped softly against the steep walls that encircled it. The well, he thought, must be fed by a spring of some sort, for the pool looked deep.

It was a strange feeling, being at the bottom of the well and he shivered slightly as he looked up at the far-away circle of dim light above his head. The distant noise of the storm echoed eerily down the shaft and as he flashed his torch over the water, he knew instinctively that this was an ancient place ... perhaps as old as time itself.

Although he hadn't consciously thought about it, Lewis had meant to kneel at the edge of the water and drink from his cupped hands. Instead, he found himself sliding forward so that he lay stretched out over the worn, old stones at the water's edge. However, even as he leant forward and plunged his face into the pool, he thought he saw a movement below the surface, the glimpse of a face that wasn't his and a swirl of water that bubbled and surged triumphantly around him. There was something in the pool!

He scrambled to his feet in panic, backing away from the edge, his breath coming in fearful, heaving gasps. He pushed a lock of wet hair from his face and stared at the rippling water in horror, wondering what nameless monster lurked in its depths.

Nothing, however, happened and as the pool returned to normal, his heart gradually stopped thumping. Nevertheless, he looked around fearfully, wondering what to do next. The trouble was that he was still thirsty for he hadn't had time to drink more than a mouthful. Dare he risk it? He moved forward and, kneeling down, slapped the surface of the water with the flat of his hand.

Nothing stirred and he relaxed as common sense told him that it could just have been his own reflection that he'd seen — and if the well was, indeed, fed by an underground spring then there was probably nothing strange in the upward surge of bubbles. Warily, he leant forward again, ready to throw himself backwards should he see anything. But there was nothing and he dipped his cupped hands into the water time after time until he could drink no more.

The pool remained calm as he got to his feet and it was only when he looked up that he realized that darkness was indeed falling. With a final glance at the pool, he turned to the rising circle of steps that wound its way upwards. Suddenly, he wanted more than anything else to be out of the confines of the well and with the torchlight cutting a bright swathe out of the darkness, he half ran and half scrambled upwards towards the fading circle of light that spelt safety.

The Arabs and the oil company rescue team arrived at Al Antara at much the same time. The storm was still raging when the camels padded up to the oasis, the sand-laden wind shrieking in fury around them as the bedouin, wrapped to the eyes in their red-checked head-gear, couched their camels among the palm trees and looked around fearfully.

"The well, Hassan," said the sheikh, his voice muffled by the tearing wind. "We'll find him by the well."

Lewis saw them through the storm and relief flooded through him for he hadn't much relished the thought of spending the entire night in the choking heat. He pulled his T-shirt from his face and stood up but even as he got to his feet, the headlights of a fleet of rescue vehicles pierced the driving, swirling sand. The sheikh lifted a warning hand and the bedouin waited by their camels as the Englishmen piled out of their vehicles and ran towards Lewis.

"Water," one of them shouted, "bring some water!"

"It's okay, Mr Williams," Lewis said. "I found the well. I'm all right!"

He sounded so cocky that Gareth Williams was sorely tempted to give him a good telling off there and then. Driving his father's car at his age! Of all the stupid idiots!

He was furiously angry but bit back his words as he glimpsed the Arabs and it was only their presence that stopped him from giving Lewis a real mouthful. Curbing his temper with an effort, he walked across to the bedouin and, recognizing old Sheikh Rashid, shook his hand.

"As salaam aleikum, Sheikh Rashid," he smiled.

Sheikh Rashid touched his forehead. *"Wa aleikum as salaam,"* came the response.

"Thank you for coming out in such weather. We appreciate your being here and I will tell Mr Grant personally of your efforts on behalf of his son."

"It's nothing," the sheikh disclaimed politely. "I saw him as he passed our tents."

"Come here, Lewis," Williams called, "and thank Sheikh Rashid for coming out in the *shimaal* to rescue you."

As Lewis stammered his gratitude, the sheikh stiffened suddenly and took a step backwards. A curious expression crossed his face and ignoring Lewis's outstretched hand, he bowed low. Very low.

Williams looked shrewdly at the old sheikh. Now what was up, he wondered. But the sheikh said nothing and the cars were waiting.

"Fii amaan illah," Williams said, unsure now as to whether to offer his hand or not.

"Fii amaan al kareem, Mr Williams," came the response and the sheikh held out his hand to him. Gareth shook it warmly and thanked the sheikh again for his help. Nice old chap, he thought, as he turned to take Lewis's arm. His lips tightened. The sooner he got him back to the township the better. Goodness knows what his father was going to say when he heard the story!

Battling the howling wind, Gareth Williams guided Lewis across the sand to the vehicles and, bundling him in, struggled round to the driver's door. The Arabs stood as he had left them, watching their departure. He gave a final wave and, slamming the door shut, took off in a swirl of dust.

Even as they left, the force of the wind seemed to quieten. Williams pondered over the old sheikh's odd behaviour as they drove back through the waning storm; their powerful headlights throwing into relief the moving, rippling sea of streaming sand that half obliterated the serrated ridges of the track. Half an hour, he reckoned, and they'd be home. Thank goodness they'd managed to find Lewis so quickly. But why had Rashid refused to shake the boy's hand?

Back at the oasis, the huddled group of bedouin watched the red rear-lights of the 4x4s disappear into the night and made to mount their beasts.

Sheikh Rashid, however, gripped his camel's halter and led the animal towards the dim outline of the ruined houses that loomed vaguely among the trees.

"Father," Hassan gasped, running after him and grabbing his sleeve. "Father, where are you going? We can't stay here at night, you know that! What about the djinn?"

His father turned and looked at them all as they stood amid the waving palms. "The djinn has gone," he said calmly. "We can now return to the village of our ancestors and sleep safely."

"But, Father," Hassan gulped, "how do you *know* the djinn has gone?"

"You have much to learn, my son," his father replied. "I looked into the eyes of that boy and the djinn looked back at me."

"So *that's* why you bowed to him as though he were a great sheikh!" Hassan said, his eyes sharpening. "I wondered at that!"

"So did Mr Williams," Sheikh Rashid smiled, "and he will wonder even more when I tell him tomorrow that we want to leave our tents and move back to Al Antara."

5. The Djinn

Robert Grant relaxed as the flight attendant removed the remains of his meal. He was completely exhausted. The Bahrain trip, he reflected, had really worn him out. Thank goodness for the chance to snatch a few hours sleep. He looked at his son who had been remarkably quiet since they'd boarded the flight. He must be missing his friends already, he decided. So many of them had called to say goodbye that they'd been late checking in.

"You all right, Lewis?" he asked casually.

"Yeah."

"It'll be nice to see your mum, won't it? I talked to her this morning. She's coming to the airport to meet us. She says she's rented a lovely house for us. It belongs to an Edinburgh professor who has gone to America for a year. It even has its own library!"

"Yeah."

His father sighed as he watched his son bury his head in a comic. Couldn't Lewis find something decent to read instead of comics? When they finally moved to Aberdeen he'd really have to be around for him more. Take him to football matches and the like; he might even take him fishing. He wanted to do all these things but the pressure of work was enormous. He'd been really angry when he'd got back that morning and Williams had told

him about the desert escapade. He sighed. Lewis
had been left to his own devices for far too long
and his grandmother's illness hadn't helped. His
wife, Margaret, had had to stay in Edinburgh to be
near the hospital and he supposed that they'd all
stay there for a few months. It might actually work
out quite well, he thought. He'd managed to get
Lewis a place at George Heriot's, his old school,
until Christmas. With any luck, he mused, he'd
have found a suitable house in Aberdeen by then.
His thoughts drifted and as unresolved problems
floated round his mind, he fell into a deep and
dreamless sleep.

Lewis lifted his eyes from his comic. He could
tell from his father's steady breathing that he was
asleep. He looked unseeingly at the back of the
chair in front of him, his face set and his eyes petrified. How it had happened, he hadn't a clue. In
fact, he couldn't believe it even now, but memories
of that morning were still vivid in his mind. He'd
been brushing his teeth and when he rinsed his
mouth and looked at the mirror he had almost died
of fright for it wasn't his own reflection that stared
back at him but the face of a rather sour-looking
old man.

"Good morning, Lewis," the man in the mirror
said. "Er … may I introduce myself? My name is
Casimir. Prince Casimir, actually."

Lewis did the first thing that came into his head.
He grabbed the bar of soap and scrubbed the mirror with it but when he wiped just a little of it off
to have a peek, he could see that the awful man
was still there.

"I'm afraid I can't be wiped away that easily, Lewis," Casimir sneered. "I'm *inside* you, you see."

"Well, get out of me," Lewis shot back at him. "I don't want you inside me! Get out, right now!"

"No, I don't think so. You see, Lewis, it suits me to live inside you."

Memories of what he had read in Peter's comic suddenly came back to him with sickening clarity. It couldn't be, surely! "A djinn!" Lewis gasped in dawning understanding. "You're a djinn!"

Casimir looked offended. "Well, sort of," he admitted. "Actually, I'm a magician," he said shortly, "but if it suits you to call me a djinn then so be it."

Lewis's mind winged its way back to the face he had glimpsed in the swirling waters of the well. "It was you, wasn't it?" he said, looking appalled. "You were in the well! I saw you in the water!"

"If you don't mind, we won't talk about the well," the face scowled fleetingly.

"What'll we talk about then? What do you want?"

"I think I want to be you, Lewis," Casimir answered gently. "You see, I need a body to live in and you are suitable in so many ways. Young, not too bright, doting family …"

"No way!" said Lewis, furious at being termed 'not too bright.' He rushed back to his room and, searching frantically through the pile of comics that he was taking with him on the flight, found the one that Peter had given him the day before. "It says here that djinns, genies, whatever you call yourself, can grant wishes. Nothing about taking people over! This is my body, I'll have you know, and I'm keeping it!"

Casimir's eyes hooded as he foresaw trouble ahead. Lewis wasn't going to be the pushover he'd thought and the last thing he wanted him to do was tell the whole story to his parents. They'd make enquiries at Al Antara and he frowned at the thought of the mistake he'd made there; for, triumphant in his freedom, he'd looked at the old sheikh through Lewis's eyes. And the sheikh had known him. Much better to compromise, he thought wisely. Make a bargain. After all, he was sure to win. No youngster could hope to outwit him. It would all come to the same thing in the end and wishes seemed as good a way as any of keeping this young hothead on a string.

"Shall we make a bargain, Lewis?" he suggested. "I will grant you one wish every day and if, by any chance, I can't do what you ask then my magic will revert to you. If *you* can't make a wish, however, I will take over your body and I will live in it for ever."

Lewis thought about it. It seemed a fair deal. There were millions of things in the world to wish for, after all, and he was quite sure that if he put his mind to it he would be able to think of something the magician couldn't do. Like moving mountains! I mean, surely this old man couldn't shift something like Mount Everest … but still …

"I don't know," he said doubtfully. "I don't really want anybody living inside me. Why don't you just get lost! Or find somebody else!"

"I'm afraid you're stuck with me for the moment, Lewis," Casimir answered, eyeing him coldly, "and, quite frankly, you'd be wise to make the best of it."

Lewis, however, still looked undecided. Casimir sighed and tried to tempt him. "You can wish for anything, you know," he reminded him. "Money, a fast car, a ..."

"What would *I* do with a fast car," Lewis said disgustedly. "I can't sit my driving test for a couple of years yet and my parents would ask me where I'd got it from."

"Well, what would you like to wish for?"

Lewis looked thoughtful. What he wanted most of all was to punish Peter, Jack and Colin for daring him to go to Al Antara in the first place. "Could you make someone ..." He had been going to say "suffer" but the sneering, knowing look in Casimir's eyes stopped him.

Now, underneath his abominable manners, Lewis was not, actually, all that bad. He was an only child, more than a bit spoiled and because his parents were always on the move job-wise, found it hard to mix and make new friends. "Could you make somebody like me?" he blurted out.

"The whole country if you like," offered Casimir obligingly.

"No, no. Just Peter, Jack and Colin and ... and ... perhaps the people at school. You know, the teachers as well."

"Done," Casimir smiled triumphantly.

And with a sinking heart, Lewis realized too late that he had been very neatly outsmarted. It was then that the phone had started to ring. It hardly stopped all morning and most of his class came to say goodbye. Peter, Jack and Colin, he thought, had been really sorry about the dare but with the djinn's magic floating round the place, he couldn't be sure if they were telling the truth. The class had given him a wonderful send off but knowing that their feelings were the result of magic, left Lewis less than impressed and looking back on it, he was furious with himself for wasting his first wish.

He shifted in his seat and sighed as he took stock of the situation. Mind you, it wasn't all bad, he reckoned. Most of the time, he forgot that the djinn was there at all for it didn't interrupt his thoughts or speak to him the whole time. In fact, it seemed that the only time he could talk to the djinn was when he was standing in front of a mirror. In this, he was totally mistaken, as he was soon to find out, but at the time he believed it and relaxed. It might, actually, work out quite well, he thought, looking on the bright side. Not everybody, after all, could have a wish granted every day. He might even have some fun!

His mother didn't stop talking from the time she met them at Edinburgh Airport till they reached the huge house she'd rented in Heriot Row. It had been pouring with rain when they'd landed and Lewis wasn't at all sure if he was going to like living in Edinburgh. He looked round. The house was grey, the street was grey and the rain was grey. Even his father felt it. "We're going to miss the sun and the sand, Lewis," he said tiredly. "And, if anything, Aberdeen is greyer than Edinburgh!"

"This is Mrs Sinclair, Bob," his mother said as the door opened. "Lewis, say hello to Mrs Sinclair, our housekeeper. She has kindly agreed to stay on while the Robinsons are in America. I've been telling Lewis," she said to the housekeeper, "that he'll have to keep his room tidy so that you don't have to climb all those stairs every day!"

"That's very kind of you, Mrs Grant," the housekeeper replied, looking dubiously at Lewis. Jeans, long, black hair and very strange eyes. She hardly heard what Mrs Grant was saying as she tried to shrug off the feeling of unease that shivered through her.

"Your room is right at the top of the house, I'm afraid, Lewis," his mother was saying apologetically. "It's a nuisance but none of these old Edinburgh houses have lifts."

Lewis looked at the housekeeper, a prim, starched-looking lady with iron-grey hair. "Don't worry about me, Mrs Sinclair," he said in his politest voice. "I'll make my own bed and keep my room clean and tidy."

Had his mother not been so anxious to keep on the right side of Mrs Sinclair, she might well have shown some suspicion at this announcement. Since when had Lewis ever lifted a duster, made his own bed or picked up his clothes?

Somehow Lewis managed to keep the smile on his face but his mind was in turmoil — for it hadn't been him that had spoken, it had been the djinn! He felt slightly sick at the thought that the djinn had been able to make him say words that weren't his own. Goodness knows what trouble that could land him in! He trembled slightly as he watched the suitcases being brought into the house, devastated by the knowledge that the djinn had more power over him than he'd thought!

Nevertheless, he quickly cottoned on to the reason for his words. If his room was at the top of the house then he reckoned that Mrs Sinclair would be more than glad to leave him well alone.

6. The Bank Robbers

"Will you mind what you're doing with that pick!" muttered Murdo irritably as Wullie wielded it with gusto.

"I've hit a tough bit," panted Wullie defensively. "A bit of wall must have fallen in and I have to break it up if we're going to get through!"

"Hit a tough bit! You nearly put a hole in my head, you great oaf!"

"Well, if you're so anxious, why don't you do a bit of the work? I'm exhausted!"

"Oh, for Pete's sake, have a break and we'll have another look at the map. There are so many of these blooming alleys that it'd be easy to pick the wrong one."

Wullie picked up one of the battery-operated lanterns and put it on a flat stone so that it shed some light on the creased sheet of yellowing paper that lay spread out over their makeshift table. With a lingering look at the inky blackness that surrounded them, he inched towards the lamp's comforting glow and reached for his cigarettes.

"Nane o' they ghosts around tonight," he muttered, lighting up and inhaling deeply. "I wonder what they're cooking up for us this time!"

Before they'd found the old map showing the network of streets that lay under the city, neither Wullie nor Murdo had believed in ghosts. After their first few sorties underground, however, this attitude had fundamentally changed. A succession of shoves, pushes and blasts of freezing cold air that had turned them blue with cold, had done much to convince them that ghosts most certainly did exist and, more to the point, had let them know quite plainly that they did not like anybody invading their territory.

Murdo had found the old map in a charity shop in Newington. Not that he usually went into charity shops, but a prowling police patrol had unnerved him and while waiting for the constables to pass, he'd nipped inside the shop and buried his head in the first big book he'd seen. The map had fallen out as he'd pulled the book off the shelf and rather than fiddle around putting it back, he'd hastily stuffed it in his carrier bag and promptly forgotten all about it until he'd got home. When he'd worked out what it was, however, he'd seen definite possibilities ... yes, very definite possibilities. So much so that, hands trembling and imagination racing wildly, he'd reached excitedly for his mobile.

"Wullie, get yerself over here right now. We might have a job on!"

They pored excitedly over the map. "Look," Murdo pointed out once they'd got it the right way round, "there's even a tunnel that goes up to the castle and if you follow it through here ... and here ... it ends up in Holyrood Palace!"

"We're going to do the Palace?" Wullie gasped, impressed.

"No, we're no' going to do the Palace, you idiot," Murdo said exasperatedly. "What's in the Palace, you clown? Nothing but auld pictures that nobody would give you tuppence for."

Having thus summarily disposed of the Queen's Collection, Murdo gave a smile of pure, unalloyed glee. "No, Wullie. Just look here. See this alley," he said, his grimy finger tracing the course of a passage that led from the cellars of Deacon Brodie's Tavern down to the outline of another imposing building on the Mound. "See where it goes!"

"Man!" Wullie looked at him in awe. "Man, that's … that's …"

"The Bank of Scotland!" crowed Murdo. "Yon passage there'll take us right into its vaults or I'm a Dutchman."

Wullie eyed Murdo questioningly. "A Dutchman?" he echoed. "I … er … I always thought you were, well, Scottish like me?" Wullie sounded confused.

Murdo gave him a look and was about to make a really cutting remark when he saw the wisdom of keeping Wullie sweet. Wullie was six feet tall and as tough as they come. He was going to need Wullie and, when the time came to blow up the vaults, probably Tammy Souter as well.

Wullie agreed. "Aye," he nodded at the mention of Tammy Souter's name. "Aye, Tammy's a good chap with a stick of dynamite. We'll get in there fine, nae bother," he said. Then he paused. "But … but didn't I read in the papers that that branch has shut down, like? It's a museum or something. Are you sure they still keep money there?" he asked anxiously.

"Trust me, Wullie!" Murdo grinned, tapping the side of his nose meaningfully.

Getting into the passages had proved a problem at first but Deacon Brodie's Tavern was always a busy place at night and as the Gents was half-way down the cellar stair they had no trouble in avoiding the brightly-lit main cellars and sneaking into an older, little used part of the building that seemed, if anything, to be a store.

"There'll be a trapdoor or something," Murdo had muttered as they looked in one room after another, all of them stacked with empty boxes and old crates. "Has to be, for these tunnels are deep."

It was Wullie who found the trapdoor in the end. By that time, they'd all but given up hope and Wullie glowed with pride at Murdo's assertion that he was a genius.

"Not just a pretty face," he agreed, shining his torch down into the blackness of the pit.

"We'll need a rope ladder or something to get down there, won't we?" Murdo muttered.

"No we won't," Willie disagreed, his mind working with unaccustomed clarity. "If we heft some of these empty crates down the hole we can easily climb down onto them. Let me go first and then you can pass the crates to me."

Clambering carefully down the rough stair that Wullie had created out of stacked crates, Murdo shone his torch into the blackness of the Underground City. The powerful beam of light lit long narrow streets with walls of crumbling brickwork and as they moved through the maze of alleys, it didn't take them long to realize that finding the right one wasn't going to be easy; for the jumble of passageways that spread in all directions seemed to bear little resemblance to their carefully drawn map. Indeed, had Murdo not remembered that the Bank of Scotland lay downhill from Deacon Brodie's Tavern, they might never have latched onto the right one at all. As it was, his eyes gleamed hopefully when they stumbled on a grim alley that sloped steeply downwards. Although it ran in the right direction, however, disappointment crossed their faces when they turned a bend and found it blocked by a fall of bricks.

Wullie looked at it, assessing the damage by the light of the torch. "It'll take weeks to shift that lot, Murdo lad," he said gloomily. "In fact, I reckon we'll be lucky to get through it by Christmas."

"There's no rush," Murdo replied. "We'll take it nice and easy. It'll take time to get picks and shovels down here for a start. We'll just play it cool. Bring in stuff bit by bit like."

The ghosts hadn't bothered them at first. Although they didn't know it, it was the old Codger who had first discovered them. He'd heard the thump of the pick and the scrape of the shovel and drifted along through alleys, dusty streets and a few solid walls to find out what was going on. It hadn't taken him long to suss them out either. He'd just hung around, listened to their chat, looked at their map and drifted off again to report to Mary King.

The ghosts had hoped that scaring tactics might work. It was, unfortunately, their only weapon, but Murdo and Wullie had proved a tough proposition. Especially Murdo! Murdo was a tough, lean, hard-bitten crook. Nothing fazed him, not even the hardest push and, while Wullie shivered with cold as the ghosts hugged him close, Murdo would cheer him up and give him what he called Dutch courage out of a flask. Wullie always accepted gratefully but to this day the involvement of the Dutch still puzzles him.

"Look, Wullie," Murdo said on one occasion when the ghosts had worn themselves to a frazzle trying to scare them, "the worst they seem to be able to do is push us around and try to freeze us solid! We'll wear more clothes tomorrow and ignore the rest. We can't see them and if that's the best they can do then we can put up with it! I'm not going to let them beat us. Just think of all the lovely lolly that's in the bank! We'll be millionaires! Now won't it be worth it, Wullie — going through all this and getting rich? You don't get millions for nothing, you know! You've got to suffer, one way or another. Nothing in this world is free!"

Wullie agreed with this sentiment wholeheartedly but it was with many a fearful glance into the darkness that he continued to shift vast piles of rubble while Murdo, heaving thick sacks of the stuff down another passage, got rid of it.

At this stage, the ghosts would probably have given up trying to get rid of Murdo and Wullie but it so happened that their prime concern wasn't really whether or not the Bank of Scotland was reduced to insolvency.

None of the ghosts ever mentioned them but they were all aware of the other inhabitants of the Underground City. The ghosts of the Plague

People! For the cellars that held them were dangerously close to where Wullie was so enthusiastically wielding his pick, and this was the real reason that the ghosts swept frantically along the tunnels every night. They were petrified that the Plague People might escape and bring the Black Death back to the streets of Edinburgh!

7. Ali Baba

Neil hurried home that afternoon, anxious to tell Clara what had happened at Mary King's Close. Graham had made such a fuss that it had taken them ages to walk all the way back down the High Street to the school. By the time they reached the gates, they'd found the playground empty and the janitor, Mr MacGregor, waiting for them.

"Right," Miss Mackenzie said, "straight to the classroom and get your bags. We're a bit late but Miss Alison will still be there when you go up."

"Thought you were never coming," MacGregor said dourly as Miss Mackenzie shepherded them through the playground towards the school door.

"Ocht, that Graham Flint's been playing me up all the way back," she said, watching as a cowed Graham, surrounded by anxious friends, made for the classroom. "Swears he was pushed by a ghost in Mary King's Close!"

MacGregor laughed, not a thing he did often. Even Miss Mackenzie grinned but she shook her head, nevertheless. "The thing is, though, that the tour guide happened to be looking at him when he hit the wall and he told me later that ... well, *he* says that *no one* pushed him!"

MacGregor's eyes sharpened. "Aye, weel! You never know," he said thoughtfully. "There've been rumours that it's haunted ever since it opened."

Neil hurried up with his bag slung over his shoulder.

"Has Clara gone home on her own, Mr MacGregor?" he asked. "I thought she might have waited for me."

"The lassie said she had a lot of homework, Neil. She'll be home by this time."

"Thanks," Neil grinned. "Bye, Miss Mackenzie!"

"He looks all right now," Miss Mackenzie said, her eyes following Neil as he made his way down the High Street towards Holyrood Palace, "but *he* was another one that was as white as a sheet in that Close. And to tell you the truth," she said, meeting MacGregor's eyes, "I didn't feel at all happy down there myself!"

Neil pulled the hood of his anorak over his head as it started to rain but as he came near his house, he almost ran the last few yards, for Sir James's car was parked outside the door and that meant news of the pantomime.

"It's on!" Clara said, rushing into the hall when she heard him open the door. *"Ali Baba's* on, Neil! Isn't that fab-u-lous!"

"Great!" Neil replied, going into the living room.

"I see you've heard the news," Sir James smiled. "Everyone is happy about it and it means that we'll still be able to raise a sizeable amount for Children's Aid."

"Which theatre is it going to be in?" asked Neil, mindful of what his mother had said. "I mean, all the big theatres have their own shows and *we* couldn't think of anywhere else big enough."

"We approached the Church of Scotland, Neil, and they have given us permission to use the Assembly Hall."

"The Assembly Hall?"

"You know, that enormous building that sits at the top of the Mound. They wouldn't normally have allowed us to put on a pantomime there but it's for charity and a very good cause!"

"When will the next rehearsal be?" asked Clara.

"Saturday evening, perhaps. We don't usually have them at the weekend, I know, but we've missed a lot of rehearsal time because of the fire. The biggest job is going to be moving all the props and costumes from The King's Theatre to the Assembly Hall."

"Were any of them damaged by the fire?" asked Mrs MacLean, who had Mischief on her lap.

"Some of the scenery was damaged, that's all. It's being replaced and they say it'll be ready in time for the opening night."

Neil jerked his head at Clara and, taking the hint, she followed him to the kitchen where he made himself a warm drink. Kitor was perched on the back of one of the kitchen chairs but fluttered to Clara's shoulder when she entered the room.

"Gosh, this is good," Neil muttered, warming his hands round the mug. "It's freezing outside!"

"How was Mary King's Close?" asked Clara. "I bet you wore your firestone!"

"Yeah," grinned Neil. "I almost wish I hadn't now. I've bags to tell you!"

"Well," asked Clara, "did you see any ghosts?"

"Dozens!" Neil said, and laughed at the disbelief on Clara's face. "I did really!"

"What ... what did they look like?" Clara asked in alarm. "Did they scare you?"

"They did, actually," admitted Neil. "They looked awful. Sort of empty eyes, you know."

"Did they know you could see them?"

"Yeah, that was the problem really ..."

"Problem?" croaked Kitor.

Neil nodded and starting from the beginning, told them everything that had happened in the Close.

"So you saw Mary King herself. What was she like?"

"Quite old, I think. She wore a sort of bonnet on her head and was quite well-dressed. You know, long skirt, blouse and a kind of thick shawl affair. I'm sure she wrote the message, 'cos she was pointing to it when it appeared."

"What did it say again?"

"Neil. We need your help. Come again. Mary King."

"You're not going to go back, though, are you?" queried Kitor anxiously.

"I might. Just to see what they want."

"They can hurt you, Neil. Look what the ghosts did to this Graham Flint that you told us about."

"There was a reason for that, though. He'd made a fool out of me and they didn't like it."

"It must have scared him though!"

"Scared him! It scared him stupid!" Neil grinned. "I told you, he was howling like a baby!"

Clara looked dubious. "You're having me on, aren't you? Graham! Crying?" she said.

Kitor flapped his wings, ruffling Clara's long, brown hair. "You shouldn't have worn your firestone," the crow said. "It was asking for trouble and now look what has happened! You're involved with ghosts!"

"Kitor's right, you know," Clara said. "What on earth do they want to see you for? You don't know their motives. They could be trying to trap you."

Neil shook his head. "I don't think so," he said. "They stuck up for me, after all. If Graham hadn't tried to make a fool of me they'd never have shoved him into a wall or frozen him half to death!"

"I wish the MacArthurs were here," sighed Clara. "We could have asked Hamish or Archie what to do."

"Why not ask your father or Sir James?" suggested Kitor reasonably.

Neil and Clara both looked at the crow in disgust. "Get a life, Kitor," Neil advised. "Ask my dad? He'd freak out!"

"Too right!" agreed Clara.

"I don't see how I'm going to be able to get into Mary King's Close, anyway," Neil said, thinking about it. "I could get in with another tour, I suppose, but it'd be expensive and the guides are sharp. They count you in and don't let you wander off."

"And at night, the whole place will be locked up …" added Clara.

"There is a way, though!" Neil said, suddenly. "I could go in on my magic carpet one afternoon after school. I'd be invisible. No one would see me."

Clara sat up. "What on earth do you mean? *You'd* go in on your magic carpet! No way are you going down into Mary King's Close on your own, Neil! I'm coming too!"

Neil looked at her doubtfully. "I don't think that's a very good idea, Clara. Really! The ghosts are a bit frightening when you see them close up. You'd be scared! I know you would!"

Kitor looked undecided for a moment. He didn't fancy going under the ground into dark streets either but he was no coward and, after all, Neil couldn't possibly be allowed to go on his own. "Don't worry, Clara," he said. "I'll go with Neil."

"Well, you can certainly come," she muttered angrily, "but if Neil goes then I'm definitely going as well!"

8. Ardray

Lewis looked at the now familiar face that confronted him in his bathroom mirror every morning. "You're nuts," he said in disbelief. "First of all, you want me to say 'carpet, carpet' and clap my hands and now you want me to open my bedroom window. Haven't you seen the weather? It's snowing outside, for goodness sake!"

"It's a request, Lewis," Prince Casimir smiled, "a request, not a command. If you would just open your window for a few minutes … to please me, Lewis!"

Lewis grinned and stuck his tongue out at the djinn before heading for the bedroom where he pulled on a pair of jeans and a sweater. Casimir seethed furiously. Just let him wait! Once he got him to Ardray, he'd soon teach him to show some respect for his elders and betters!

"If my mother comes in and finds the window open, I'm in trouble," Lewis said aloud, knowing that the djinn could hear him. "The central heating's on full blast, you know!" Nevertheless, he went to one of the windows and, hooking his fingers through the old-fashioned brass rings, pulled the window up. Six inches was enough. The magic carpet that had been hovering outside almost knocked him on his back as it flew in on the icy blast that whistled through the room.

Lewis scrambled to his feet, pushed the window down and stomped into the bathroom so that he could speak to Casimir face to face. "You might have told me you were expecting a magic carpet!" he said in annoyance. "It gave me the fright of my life!"

Casimir, however, was still dizzy with relief at the return of his carpet! It had answered his call. Now he could go home. Home to Ardray!

"That little mirror we bought yesterday, Lewis. Look into it, will you, so that I can talk to you in the bedroom and tell you about my carpet."

Lewis nodded and went to fetch the mirror, wondering why he had ever been worried at the thought of having a djinn inside him, for he had not only become accustomed to living with Casimir, he was actually feeling grateful to him. So far, he had to admit, the djinn had more than kept his side of the bargain.

When he'd woken up to his first morning in Edinburgh, his first wish had been for cash. He was quite sure that Edinburgh would have all the big music stores and as he was desperate to bring his CD collection up to date, he'd asked for a hundred pounds. Casimir, however, had suggested a thousand. A hundred pounds, he'd advised, didn't go far nowadays. The bundles of five pound notes that had then thumped down on the bathmat made Lewis blink and, worried that Mrs Sinclair might prowl round upstairs to see if he really was keeping his room tidy, he had gathered them up and hurriedly locked them in his suitcase.

As it turned out, he hadn't been able to go shopping that morning as his parents had taken him with them to the hospital to visit his Gran. The hospital was huge and when Lewis got to the ward, he found it hard to believe that his kind, friendly grandmother had turned into the frail, shrunken old lady lying in the narrow bed. The change in her had frightened him and his face had been thoughtful as he'd left the hospital.

The next morning he'd asked Casimir anxiously if he could make his Gran better. Casimir's lips tightened and he gave Lewis a most peculiar look. What Lewis didn't know was that in the world of magic, Casimir was generally regarded as being proud, arrogant and aloof by his fellow magicians. Indeed, his opinion of himself was so high that he very rarely deigned to speak to anyone less well-bred than himself. He was certainly *not* the type to be involved in good deeds, neither was he prone to being charitable; rather the opposite, if the truth be told. Casimir, therefore, was a good deal taken aback to find that Lewis quite naturally expected him to behave with compassion.

A bargain, however, was a bargain and Casimir was not ignoble. So he'd looked at Lewis strangely and said that it'd take some time but that yes, he could make his Gran better. And that afternoon, Lewis found his mother in the living room, her eyes shining with hope. The hospital had just phoned to say that his Gran was responding surprisingly well to new drugs and that she seemed set to recover.

Lewis, therefore, was feeling really grateful to the djinn and went quite happily into the bedroom where he found the magic carpet draped over one of the radiators, steaming gently. He looked at it dismissively for although he knew it was a magic carpet it was, as far as he was concerned, certainly nothing to write home about. It was a pitiful thing, really, he thought; thin, patched and almost threadbare in places. He could see from Casimir's face in the mirror, however, that he was really upset at the state of the carpet.

"What happened?" Casimir asked the carpet, his voice choked with emotion. "What happened to you?"

Lewis didn't understand half of the story that poured from the carpet. What on earth, he wondered, were storm carriers and who were Prince Kalman and Lord Rothlan?

Casimir's face was a picture for he was looking totally devastated, furiously angry and filled with concern for his carpet, all at the same time. Lewis lifted it from the radiator. He could see from the colours and the weave that it must, at one time, have been a beautiful carpet. Now, however, its colours were faded, it was patched in several places and its silken threads were so thin as to be threadbare.

He looked at Casimir in the little mirror. "Look," he said, "I haven't had my wish today and since it means so much to you, my wish is that your carpet will be made new again."

Casimir looked at Lewis blankly. As a powerful magician, he wasn't exactly used to being on the receiving end of simple, everyday acts of kindness and Lewis's words rather took him aback. Then, as their import hit home, his expression cleared and, too full of emotion to speak, he merely nodded.

Lewis felt the carpet stir under his fingers and watched in amazement as it started to thicken perceptibly. Its colours brightened and grew stronger and its silken threads gleamed and shone in the light of his bedside lamp. When it was whole again, the carpet rippled with joy and took off round the room, whizzing around in circles until it forgot itself completely and wrapped itself round Lewis in sheer joy.

"How would you like to take a trip on the carpet?" Casimir asked, his usually sour face smiling and happy. "After you've had your breakfast, that is."

"Won't people see me?"

Casimir shook his head. "It's a magic carpet," he said, "and as you'll be travelling with me inside you, you'll be invisible!"

Lewis thought about it. "I could," he said. "Mum and Dad are going back to the hospital today and then visiting some aunt or other."

"Then we'll wait until they've left. How's that?"

"Great," Lewis said, and went downstairs feeling happier than he had for a long time.

Flying on the carpet was cold, but fun. It hadn't needed Casimir to tell him that it was freezing outside for Edinburgh, covered in an unseasonably early fall of snow, had turned into a fairytale city overnight. At Casimir's suggestion, he'd spread a blanket over the carpet to keep it warm and put on a couple more sweaters. Now, zipped up in his anorak with the hood pulled tightly round his face he peered over the edge of the carpet as they passed over Princes Street, the snowy ramparts of Edinburgh Castle and the turreted splendour of George Heriot's School. He looked at it with interest, for once the October holiday finished he would be going there for the remainder of the term. His mother had already bought him the uniform! The snow-covered slopes of the Meadows floated by underneath the carpet and then more houses but it was only when they crossed the City Bypass and continued to head north that Lewis realized that it was not just taking him for a short flight round the city. He fished in a pocket and brought out the small mirror.

"Where are we going?" he asked anxiously, as Casimir's face appeared. "Where are you taking me?"

"We're going to visit my house," Casimir said, soothingly.

"Where is it? Is it far?"

"Quite a long way. I should have told you, I know, but I haven't been there for hundreds of years and, well ... I'd like to see what it's like now."

There wasn't much Lewis could say to this but if the magician had a house of his own that was miles away from Edinburgh, he saw future problems looming and as the hours passed and the carpet showed no signs of slowing down, he started to get really worried.

"Casimir," he demanded, "is it much further? At this rate it'll be dark by the time we get back to Edinburgh! My mum and dad will freak! Especially after what happened at Al Antara. I don't want to get into any more trouble if I can possibly avoid it!"

"Almost there," Casimir promised, but it was actually a good half hour before the carpet lost height and started to circle a snow-covered mountainside.

Lewis fished out the mirror again. "Are we here?" he asked. "I don't see any houses."

Casimir looked over the slopes of the bleak mountain and spoke, through Lewis, to the carpet which started to circle the area very slowly. Then it stopped.

"Get off the carpet and move forward, Lewis. Slowly! Hold your hands out in front of you and stop when you touch something."

"But ... but there's nothing to touch," Lewis said. "The mountain's ..." He stopped suddenly as his hand touched something invisible that sent a shock through him. "I'm touching something, Casimir. It's ..." he moved his hand and walked round the object, "it's like a pillar. Look, my footprints have made a circle in the snow."

Casimir looked through Lewis's eyes at the carpet. "Where did you come from, if it wasn't from Ardray?" he asked.

The carpet trembled. "Old Agnes mended me," it said. "Prince Kalman asked me what had happened when you were fleeing from the storm carriers and ... and I told him. But he didn't keep me. He didn't need to, master. He has his own carpet. So I stayed with Agnes. Master, I didn't know that this had happened to Ardray, I swear it! If she knew, she didn't tell me!"

"What *has* happened to Ardray?" interrupted

Lewis. "Isn't your house here any more?"

"My house and estates have been destroyed," Casimir said. "This ... this pillar of energy that you touched is all that is left of them."

"Was it ... *magicked?*" Lewis asked curiously.

"You could call it that," Casimir said, looking old, tired and decidedly worried. "There's only one way to find out. We'll get the carpet to fly around and see if we can spot any goblins. There might be some left lurking around to tell us what went on!"

The carpet took off again and this time flew high among the snowy peaks. Lewis hugged himself as the biting cold chilled him to the bone.

"There," Casimir said. "That's a goblin's cave if ever I saw one!"

The carpet hovered outside the cave and Lewis retched at the foul, disgusting smell that came from it. He'd never met a goblin before and wasn't particularly anxious to meet one now. But, since Casimir was inside him, he had no choice but to go into the cave holding the mirror in front of him. The place stank to the heavens and Lewis would have given anything to be able to turn round and leave. From the mirror, Casimir spoke magic words in a strange voice and, from the back of the cave there was a rustling and heaving as a ghastly crea-ture rose from its dark depths and moved into the dim light that filtered in from outside. Lewis felt sick. The goblin was green and totally revolting, with gleaming red eyes, sharp teeth and claws. It smelt foul and was covered in sagging folds of knob-bly, papery skin that rustled as it moved.

"Tell me!" Casimir demanded from the mirror.

"Tell me what happened at Ardray!"

The goblin stared in blank amazement at Casimir's face in the mirror. "Prince Casimir!" it slavered, gnashing sharp teeth. "You have returned!"

"As you see," snapped the prince.

The goblin bowed and grovelled in front of him. "Ardray is no more, Master," it said sorrowfully.

"Tell me about it!" demanded Casimir. "At once!"

The goblin fawned at his feet in a stinking rustle of flesh. "Your son, Prince Kalman, found the Sultan's Crown and kept it here in the room of mirrors but Lord Rothlan and the Turkish Sultan came and took it from him."

"You were there?"

"Yes, master. I saw the Sultan take the crown from the Prince. Rothlan's eagle, Amgarad, attacked him and he tried to escape through one of the mirrors."

"And?"

"It was locked on the other side, Master. They trapped him between mirrors and Ardray shook with the violence of it. I was lucky to get away before it disintegrated altogether."

Casimir's face suddenly grew strained and old. He looked at the goblin. "You don't happen to know where the mirror was set for, do you?"

"Oh, yes, Master. There was never any secret about it," the goblin looked surprised. "We all knew that the mirrors were set for Edinburgh!"

9. Shades of the Past

A howling blizzard had blown throughout the night and as Neil and Clara sailed up the High Street on their magic carpets, skimming between the white roofs of the picturesque old houses, they looked around in wonder. It was like fairyland. The whole of Edinburgh lay deep in drifts of snow that glinted crisp and white in the thin rays of a wintry sun.

Kitor shivered on Clara's shoulder and shifted on his claws as she fastened the top button of her coat and stuck her gloved hands in her pockets. Although she couldn't see him, she knew her magic carpet was following Neil's and as it soared above a double-decker bus she crossed her fingers and hoped that their plan would work and they'd be able to get into the Close unseen.

When they reached the City Chambers, her carpet hovered uncertainly and then headed for the broad, arched passageway that led to the entrance. Despite the weather, Mary King's Close seemed quite busy, with one or two huge, tourists buses parked outside. Clara watched as the swing-door suddenly swung open and then closed again. Good, she thought. That means Neil's inside. Now it's my turn. Choosing a time when the doorway was empty of people, Clara's carpet sailed down so that she, too, could slip inside. It wasn't quite plain sailing, however, and she had to hang on to her carpet as it suddenly tipped sideways to avoid a couple of teenagers. Kitor squawked in alarm as he dug his claws into her coat to keep his balance and some heads turned at the sudden noise but, as Kitor was invisible, they could see nothing. Clara sighed with relief. At least they were inside! Her carpet sailed round the entrance hall where people were clustered either waiting for the next tour to start or just wandering round looking at the displays and items for sale in the shop.

"Hang on, Kitor," she whispered to the crow as one of the tour guides, dressed in old-fashioned clothes, got his tour group together and opened the door. "We're heading for the stairs!" As the carpet tilted forward steeply, she leant back, grabbing at its sides to help her keep her balance as it sailed down into the depths of the earth.

Once in the network of old rooms and cellars, she looked around interestedly and then gulped in horror for, just as Neil had done, she saw the ghosts at once. She felt Kitor's claws dig into her shoulders and knew that he was probably just as scared of them as she was.

Her carpet floated through a window into the Close itself and as they drifted here and there, following Neil's carpet, Clara realized that he was probably looking for Mary King. Time passed and still they circled over the heads of tourists and ghosts alike. Then she heard Neil's voice close to her. "Clara, I can't see her anywhere! I'm going to ask one of the ghosts to fetch her. I'll get off the carpet so that they can see me!"

"Be careful, Neil!" she warned. "It won't only be the ghosts that'll be able to see you!"

Neil slipped off his carpet and stood right in front of an elderly ghost wearing a wig, knee breeches and a brocaded coat. He looked right into the ghost's empty eyes and said briefly. "My name's Neil. I was here before. I've come to speak to Mary King."

Clara giggled and then clapped a hand over her mouth to stifle the noise. Usually ghosts scare people but Neil had obviously given this ghost the fright of its life! It stepped hastily into a brick wall and then stuck its head back through to see if Neil was still there.

"Go on, then! Fetch her!" Neil said to the astounded ghost. "I can't stand here all day!" And to the ghost's amazement he got back on his carpet and disappeared.

Mary King arrived a few minutes later and looked around suspiciously. Again Neil clambered off his carpet and she jerked backwards at his sudden appearance. "We can't talk here," he said quickly. "I'll see you down at the end of the Close."

Word had obviously spread among the ghosts that something quite out of the ordinary was happening and Clara watched in horror as they started to drift from windows, walls and houses in their hundreds. She soared above them, quite invisible on her carpet, for they had agreed before-hand that only Neil would show himself to the ghosts. Peering over its edge, she looked in awe at the fearsome, ghastly crowd that followed Mary King to the end of the Close.

Neil got off his carpet and promptly wished he hadn't, for the sea of faces that confronted him wasn't the least bit friendly.

"Are you one of the magic people?" Mary King asked abruptly, her face set and angry.

Neil dug his nails into the palms of his hands to stop himself from trembling and shook his head. "No, I'm not," he said.

"How come you have a magic carpet then?" queried another ghost, pushing its way to the front of the crowd. "In this city it's only the MacArthurs that have carpets! Are you one of them?"

"No, but I know them. That's how I have a carpet."

The crowd gave an angry growl.

"Look," Neil said, cross with himself at feeling so scared and suddenly fed up with the lot of them, *"you* asked me to come here. *You* said you needed my help. Well, here I am! What's all this about?"

Good for you, Neil! Clara thought, cheering him on.

A youngish man wearing a wig spoke slowly. "Maybe he doesn't know."

"You're right," Neil said shortly. "I don't know! That's why I'm here!"

"What Mr Rafferty means, Neil," explained Mary King, "is that magic people have a bad effect on us. We, er ... tend to lose our substance and fade away if we're in contact with them."

"Which we'd rather not do," Clarinda chipped in pertly. "Being a ghost is better than nothing, you know!"

"I'm sure it is," Neil said uncertainly, "but you don't need to worry about me. I'm not a MacArthur,

I'm just a boy and … and I'll help you if I can."

The ghosts relaxed noticeably at this and even Mary King's face softened. "Well," she began, in a friendlier tone of voice, "that's all right then! I'd better begin by telling you what's been happening here! It's like this. Some time ago, the old Codger here," she indicated an old man, who raised his hand in a brief salute, "found two men in the tunnels below Deacon Brodie's Tavern. They had a map of the Underground City with them and were trying to clear some of the roads. From what they say … well, we think they're bank robbers!"

"Bank robbers?" Neil said in complete surprise. Whatever else he'd expected to hear, it certainly hadn't been that.

"The Bank of Scotland," nodded the old Codger. "Just down the road. They're going to blow up the vaults and steal a million pounds!"

"You mean … you want me to tell the police and have them arrested?" Neil said.

"No, no," burst out another of the ghosts. "No more people! That's the last thing we want!"

"I see," Neil said weakly, not understanding in the slightest, "but if you don't want me to tell the police, what *do* you want me to do?"

"We want you to tell them to go away!" Mr Rafferty said seriously. "We've tried everything, Neil. We've tried to freeze them out, we've pushed them around and nothing has made the slightest bit of difference. They still come every night to clear the rubble!"

"There's no way that we can get through to them, you see," interrupted the old Codger with a shake of his head, "they can't *see* us and they can't *hear* us!"

"So we thought," Mary King said, "that since *you* can see us and hear us that ... well, *you* might be able to speak to them for us."

"We'll show you the way through the tunnels to where they're working, no problem," Mr Rafferty said encouragingly. "And bring you back!"

Neil looked at them, a frown crossing his face. "I *could* talk to them, I suppose," he admitted. "They wouldn't be able to see me or the magic carpet but they *would* be able to hear me. Mind you," he said, looking doubtful, "if they really are bank robbers, I don't think it'll honestly make much difference *what* I say. Bank robbers are a tough lot and believe me, they're not going to give up a million pounds just because I ask them to clear out! Besides, I doubt if that bank has any money in it at all, you know. My dad told me that it's not a branch any more. Nowadays, it's a museum."

"What do you think we should do, then?"

Neil shrugged. "Well, you don't have to do anything, really, do you," he pointed out. "It's just a matter of time. Once they find out that there's no money in the bank, they'll go away anyway, won't they?"

There was a fearful silence. Mr Rafferty started to wring his hands and the rest of the ghosts moaned horribly and eyed one another sideways, suddenly scared stiff.

Neil looked at them, sensing the fear that coloured the atmosphere. "That isn't the real reason you want rid of them, is it?" he said apprehensively.

"There's something else, isn't there? Something you haven't told me!"

Mary King pleated her skirt with nervous fingers. "Yes," she admitted. "You see, we ... we aren't alone down here in the Underground City. There are places where *we* don't go ... where ... *other* ghosts live."

"The ghosts of the Plague People," Mr Rafferty burst out nervously. "They were sealed in their cellars hundreds of years ago but they've always been desperate to escape. They long to be free again," he whispered hoarsely, his voice trembling, "to roam in the open air! To infect people! To give them the Black Death!"

Clara sat, round-eyed and horrified on her carpet while Neil swallowed hard and turned the colour of chalk. "The plague?" he breathed fearfully.

Mary King nodded. "They carry the plague with them and the two men, Murdo and Wullie, are very close to their cellars, Neil. They might break into them by mistake. You must tell them the danger they're in for, if the Plague People get out, *they* will be their first victims!"

"Of course I'll tell them," Neil said immediately. "Right now, if you like!"

Mary King shook her head. "They're not there just now," she said. "Murdo and Wullie only ever come at night."

Neil looked troubled. "I can't come at night," he said slowly. "I just can't! If I'm out, I have to be home by seven at the latest. I know I could get in here before they lock up but, if I did, I wouldn't be able to get out again until they opened the doors in the morning! My parents ..." Neil tailed off, shuddering at the thought of what his mother and father would say.

"The men get in and out through the cellars of Deacon Brodie's Tavern" the old Codger offered, passing a hand over his grizzled chin, thoughtfully. "Couldn't you get in and out the same way?"

Neil grinned weakly as he shook his head. "They'd never let me into Deacon Brodie's Tavern," he said. "I'm not nearly old enough. No, we'll have to think of something else!"

10. Tracksuit and Trainers

"Have you ever been jogging, Lewis?" Casimir asked one morning.

Lewis looked at him suspiciously. It hadn't taken him long to realize that Casimir's words always had a purpose of some sort behind them. Jogging, however, seemed a fairly safe subject so he answered truthfully. "Yes, of course I have," he replied. "Why do you ask?"

"I thought we might go jogging this morning, that's all," was the reply.

"In this weather!" exclaimed Lewis, looking out of the window. The snow had melted away but it was still quite a blustery day and the trees in the gardens opposite were blowing in the wind.

"Come on, Lewis," cajoled Casimir. "The exercise will do you good!"

"Yeah, I suppose ..." Lewis said reluctantly. He might as well go jogging, he thought, for he had nothing much else to do. He wasn't due to start at his new school until Monday morning and life had been a bit dull since the magic carpet episode.

He frowned slightly as he looked back on it, for no one had made a fuss about his late return. Maybe old Casimir had had something to do with that, he thought. But, certainly, his parents and starchy, old Mrs Sinclair just hadn't seemed to have missed him. When he'd gone down to the kitchen to make some hot toast, absolutely frozen after the journey back, they'd said goodnight to him as though he'd been in his room all evening!

Nor, which was more to the point, had they noticed the painting of the *Mona Lisa* either, although he'd hung it above the mantelpiece in the library rather than in his room. Bit of a waste of a wish that had been, he thought resentfully. He'd been looking through some of the books in the library and come across one that had really taken his fancy. It was full of pictures of fabulous jewels, gold statues, Persian carpets and famous paintings — including the *Mona Lisa*. Knowing that it was the most famous painting in the world, he'd made it his wish for the day and been absolutely gutted when Casimir had produced it. He'd have sent it back the next day if it hadn't meant wasting a wish. As far as he was concerned, it was awful — dark, dingy and the woman wasn't even beautiful! What people saw to rave about, he just couldn't imagine.

His father raised his eyebrows as Lewis appeared in his tracksuit at the breakfast table. He was pleasantly surprised.

"Going jogging, Lewis?"

Resisting the temptation to say "No, I'm going to swim across the Forth," Lewis grunted as he helped himself to toast and marmalade. Shocked at his bad manners, Casimir said hastily, "I thought I'd run round Arthur's Seat. Lots of people do it and it's good training!"

His mother nodded approvingly as she buttered a piece of toast. "Bit chilly to go jogging, isn't it?" she remarked. "Mind and wrap up well!"

"Arthur's Seat!" his father said, looking at him with respect as he put his cup in its saucer and pushed it to one side. "Well done, Lewis. I'm glad to see that you're keeping fit." His eyes twinkled. "Planning to get in the school rugby team are you?"

As he was as thin as a rake, this was obviously the kind of grown-up joke that adults found funny. Lewis, furious that Casimir had butted into the conversation, was about to mutter something unintelligible when he caught his father's eye. Whether it was because Casimir was inside him, making him more perceptive than usual, he didn't know, but he suddenly felt the weight of his father's responsibilities. He bent his head over his plate as it dawned on him that being an adult and holding down a tough job wasn't all that much fun.

"Come off it, Dad!" he muttered, taking charge of the conversation. "Do I really look like a rugby player?" Then he added with a touch of shyness. "I might go in for athletics, though."

His father looked at him thoughtfully. "You'd probably do well in athletics," he nodded. "You've the build of a runner. Well," he said, folding his paper and laying it on his plate, "if you're set on jogging round the park would you like me to give you a lift? I've a meeting there this morning."

"In the park?" Lewis's mother looked surprised.

"Close by. An old school chum owns a distillery there, down by the palace. He's putting on a pantomime for Children's Aid and I've managed to persuade the company to make quite a sizeable donation."

"Free tickets then?" grinned Lewis, suddenly interested. "Which one are they putting on?"

"Ali Baba and the Forty Thieves. Actually, I don't know how you feel about pantomimes now that you're older but I've a mind to see it. He's managed to get that new comedian, Matt Lafferty, to star in it."

"Sounds great," Lewis agreed. "And Mum would enjoy it, too," he added hastily, before Casimir could butt in. "I know that Gran's on the mend but Mum really needs cheering up, don't you, Mum?" He grinned across the table at his mother who looked quite touched.

Robert Grant looked at his son in surprise. "It's nice of you to be so concerned, Lewis. We've been through a worrying time lately and quite frankly I think the panto would do us all good."

At that moment, Mrs Sinclair came in to clear the breakfast table and as his father got to his feet, Lewis picked up the morning paper, for the words *"Mona Lisa"* had caught his eye. He unfolded the paper and stared at it in horror. The headlines in *The Scotsman* screamed at him from across the front page. "Mystery of the Missing *Mona Lisa,"* "Theft at the Louvre," *"Mona Lisa* Vanishes!" He gulped as he followed his father out to the car. Just wait until he got Casimir on his own! Just wait!

Casimir, however, had no sympathy for him. "What did you expect?" he snapped. "You wished for the *Mona Lisa* and I gave it to you. What more do you want?"

Lewis, by then, was jogging along the side of Dunsapie Loch, high in Arthur's Seat. "I didn't mean you to *steal* it!" he said, looking into the mirror that nestled in the palm of his hand.

Casimir glared back at him. "Grow up, Lewis! You got what you wished for and I've hexed the painting so that no one will ever give it more than a passing glance."

Lewis looked doubtful. "You mean they'll take it for a print?" he queried.

"Whatever," muttered Casimir. *"I'm* not stupid, even if you are! Do you really think I want the police knocking on your front door? You're quite safe and that's the end of it!"

Relief flooded through Lewis. "Thank goodness!" he said. "You should have *seen* the headlines in the papers!"

"I *did* see the headlines in the papers," Casimir snapped. "I read them with you!"

"You mean you can see through my eyes?" Lewis wasn't too sure if he was happy at the thought or not.

"Of course I can. Now give over, Lewis, there's something I want you to do for me."

"What's that?" Lewis asked apprehensively.

"Nothing drastic! I want you to leave this road and climb to the top of Arthur's Seat."

"Why?" asked Lewis. "If it's a view of Edinburgh you want then there's one just round the corner."

"I don't want a view of Edinburgh, Lewis," Casimir snapped irritably. "Just do as you're told, for once!"

The slope was steep with patches of snow lying here and there on the ground. Lewis muttered under his breath, more worried about keeping his

trainers clean than doing what Casimir wanted
and was glad when the magician called a halt.
"Now, Lewis, hold the mirror in front of you and
go carefully!"

Lewis, remembering the pillar of magic he had
found in Ardray, moved steadily upwards and then
came to a halt. He held his hands out and tried to
take another step forward and just couldn't. It was
as though an invisible curtain lay between him and
the summit of the hill. "It's the strangest thing,"
he said to Casimir in a puzzled voice. "There's
something in the way and I don't seem to be able
to go any further. There's nothing that I can see to
stop me, but ... I just can't move forward."

"That's all I wanted to know," Casimir said in
a tired voice. "The MacArthurs have put a protective shield round the hill."

"Who on earth are the MacArthurs?" asked
Lewis, turning thankfully to make his way down
towards the loch again.

"They're a magic people who live inside Arthur's
Seat. I want to talk to them."

"About your son, Prince Kalman?" asked Lewis
sympathetically, glancing at Casimir's face in the
little mirror. Casimir, however, was deep in thought
and didn't answer. In a way, he was quite glad that
the magic shield had stopped Lewis in his tracks
for he hadn't really decided what he was going
to say to the MacArthur when they met. And the
more he thought about it, the more of a problem it
became. For how could he possibly justify the theft
of the Sultan's crown to the MacArthur? The long
and the short of it was that he couldn't. The whole

thing was absolutely ridiculous and yet, even after the hundreds of years he had spent mouldering in the well at Al Antara, he could still remember the overwhelming urge that had possessed him. Mind and body had been filled with greed for the crown and its power. And Kalman had been the same. They must both have been mad, he thought grimly. There could be no other explanation. What on earth had possessed him to go to such lengths?

Flying high above the hill, Kitor flew on his daily patrol over Arthur's Seat. He didn't have to do it but he felt that it helped the Ranger and was a small return for making him part of his family. So, if any of the sheep strayed or got themselves caught on the crags, he let the Ranger know and, with the MacArthurs on holiday in Turkey, he also kept an eye open for trouble from the world of magic. Although this was always a possibility, it was, nevertheless, remote and the last thing Kitor had expected were problems from that particular quarter. He was, therefore, stunned when Lewis was quite obviously stopped in his tracks by the protective shield that the MacArthurs had left round the hill.

Kitor watched through narrowed eyes as the boy left the slopes and continued to jog round the park towards the exit. He knew perfectly well that the protective shield round the hill only kept out magicians, but this lad — tall, thin and lanky — certainly didn't look like any sort of magician that he'd ever met. The fact, however, remained that he'd tried to get through the shield and hadn't been able to. Kitor flapped to the branches of a nearby tree and, nerves alert, watched and waited. He was most definitely going to follow this strange boy home.

11. Prince of Thieves

"Well! Did you find a way in this time?" Kitor asked excitedly as Neil and Clara came home from the Assembly Hall where rehearsals for *Ali Baba* were in full swing.

"No," Neil said, opening the fridge to get a drink, "the doors to the cellars are still locked but we might have a chance to get into them in a couple of days time! I heard the producer say that they're going to have to use them to store all the props and things that are coming from The King's."

It was Clara who had had the brilliant idea. The Assembly Hall building, she had pointed out to Neil, stood at the top of the Mound. And if the cellars from Deacon Brodie's Tavern gave on to the Underground City then it was more than likely that they could get down to it through the cellars in the Assembly Hall as well. Although it had seemed a sensible plan, however, it had come to nothing for, as Neil had said, all the doors leading to the basement had been locked and, with no idea where the keys were kept, they hadn't been able to do anything.

"What about you, Kitor," asked Clara, pushing her hair behind her ears, "did you have any luck with that boy?"

"He's started school now," Kitor informed them. "His mother picked him up afterwards and they went to the hospital to visit his grandmother. They go there most afternoons. His name is Lewis, by the way. I heard his mother telling him to go back into the house and get his PE kit."

"He doesn't sound much like a magician to me," Neil frowned. "Are you sure he was trying to get through the MacArthur's protective shield?"

Kitor nodded his head. "Quite sure," he croaked.

"I wish the MacArthurs would come back," Clara said with a sigh. "I really miss them."

It wasn't only Clara who was missing the MacArthurs, however. Sir James and the Chief Constable of Edinburgh were missing them, too. As they stood chatting together in the windows of the New Club, overlooking Princes Street Gardens and the wintry bulk of Edinburgh Castle, it was the Chief Constable who brought the subject up.

"I've been meaning to have a word with you for a while, James," Archie Thompson said, "about the MacArthurs."

Sir James looked at him in surprise. "The MacArthurs? They're still in Turkey aren't they?"

"You don't, by any chance, know when they'll be back, do you?"

Sir James shook his head. "I'm afraid not," he replied. "Er ... I don't want to pry, but is something bothering you?"

"You could say that," the Chief Constable said, eyeing him sourly. "It's all these art thefts that are taking place round the world."

"All what art thefts?" queried Sir James, startled. "I heard that the *Mona Lisa* had been stolen and there was something about a famous emerald but ..."

"That's all that's been released to the public, James. The rest has been kept quiet."

Sir James raised his eyebrows. "The rest?" he queried.

"Yes, there have been quite a few other robberies that haven't reached the pages of the newspapers."

"For any specific reason?"

"It's not so much the things that have been stolen, James, it's the manner of the thefts. You see, all the stuff that's been taken from art galleries, museums and the like — well, the pieces have literally just disappeared. No signs of forced entry, no trace of the thieves ... nothing whatsoever."

"But what about the security cameras and alarm systems? They're supposed to be foolproof these days, aren't they?"

"That's what's worrying us. The alarms go off when the pieces are stolen but the security cameras show nothing out of the ordinary. The *Mona Lisa,* for instance — well, it just disappeared from the wall. Apparently, the camera footage was amazing. One minute the painting was there and the next minute it had gone. Nobody went near it."

"Don't you have you any idea who might have taken it? A rogue collector wanting to add to his collection perhaps?"

"If it were a collector," Archie Thompson stated positively, "the chances are that he'd steal more of the same kind. Someone with a collection of paintings would steal more paintings, someone with a collection of jewels would steal more jewels. That hasn't happened. Everything that's been stolen is different — a painting, a jewel, an ivory, a sculpture and so on. Interpol's going crazy, every antique dealer in the world is on the lookout for them but so far nobody has come up with anything. It's mind-boggling! I've no idea who this fellow is but he certainly ranks as a Prince of Thieves."

"And what's gone missing from Scotland that you're so het up about?" asked Sir James with a slight smile. "The Crown Jewels?"

Archie Thompson looked at him grimly and turned pale. "Don't even think about it, James! Nothing's safe these days and the very idea gives me nightmares!" He heaved a sigh. "No, the thing is, I had a letter this morning from the National Museum of Scotland. They're hosting an exhibition of priceless diamonds during the Festival next summer and the thought of policing it ... well, it's making me sweat already! I wondered ... well, if it does take place, I wondered if I could ask the MacArthur or Lord Rothlan to put a protective shield around the exhibits. Unofficially, needless to say! Like Prince Kalman did last year with the Sultan's Crown. What do you think?"

"I'm sure they would, but what makes you think the diamonds would be a target, Archie?"

"The strangest thing of all about the robberies is that every piece that's been stolen appears in a book called *Famous Collections of the World,* and two of the largest diamonds in the exhibition are shown in it. At the moment, Interpol is trying to trace everyone who bought a copy."

"That's a bit of a tall order, isn't it?"

"Not that tall, James. It's a limited edition and only five hundred copies were printed."

As it happened, one of the five hundred copies of *Famous Collections of the World* lay open just a couple of hundred yards away ... on Lewis's bed!

Lewis was deep in thought as he flicked through the pages. "I think I might wish for this painting next," he said to Casimir. "It's by Picasso and although it's an odd sort of painting, there's something about it that I like. What do you think?"

Casimir looked at the painting and reserved his judgment. Yet it was in the book so he presumed that Lewis was right in his assessment. "You've wished for a painting already, Lewis," he reminded him.

"Yes, and what a wash-out *that* was!" Lewis muttered.

"The thing is," Casimir said diffidently, "that you're only allowed to wish for something once. You can't wish for another painting!"

Lewis sat up and looked at Casimir in the little mirror. "What do you mean, I can't wish for another painting?" he said. "You didn't tell me anything about that when we made our agreement!"

"You didn't ask," Casimir pointed out.

"But ..."

"One of a kind, Lewis!" And Lewis knew from the look on his face that Casimir would never relent. He threw the mirror across the room and the book after it but even as he did so, he was gripped by a deadly fear. "One of a kind" cut down his choices considerably. It wouldn't be long, he thought, before he ran out of things to wish for. And then what?

He looked dismally round his room. It wasn't a bedroom any more, really. It was a miniature palace containing a treasure trove of all the beautiful things he had wished for: a Chinese carpet hung on the wall; a huge, carved emerald glowed green on an ebony stand; a tall ivory statue gleamed delicately from a corner and many other priceless objects decorated shelves and the top of his bookcase. Tears gathered in his eyes. He loved them all.

He left the mirror lying face down on the carpet and picked up the book. His face was white and strained as he went slowly downstairs to the library and put it back where he had found it. As he did so, he glimpsed the picture of the *Mona Lisa* smiling down at him from above the fireplace. Her smile had subtly altered and he instinctively knew its meaning. He had been right to dislike the painting for her smile was a sly smile; a nasty, sly, knowing smile that seemed to take pleasure in his desperation.

"What am I going to do?" Lewis whispered to the empty room. "What on earth am I going to do?"

12. Police Probe

Saturday morning! Lewis stretched lazily in bed, enjoying the luxury of a long lie. He'd actually quite enjoyed his first week at school; his teacher was great and the boys and girls had been friendly. He had piles of homework to do, of course, but so far the worst thing about it was having to get up at the crack of dawn when it was still pitch black outside. Idly he got out of bed and was heading for the shower when he heard the doorbell ring. As his mother and father had gone house hunting in Aberdeen he slipped out of his room and peered over the banister to see who the visitor was. He turned white with shock, for two uniformed police officers were standing in the hall talking to Mrs Sinclair. Her voice floated clearly up the stairwell.

"Yes, the house *does* belong to Mr Robinson," she was saying, "but he went to America in the summer. It's rented out just now to a Mr and Mrs Grant, but I'm afraid they're not in at the moment. They went up to Aberdeen yesterday."

One of the policemen produced a piece of paper. "It was actually Mr Robinson we wanted to see," one of them said. "We're checking on a book that he bought last year. It's called *Famous Collections of the World*. I wonder if we could have a look at it?"

"That's no bother at all, officer," Mrs Sinclair said, relieved that the matter wasn't serious. "If it's any-where, it'll be in the library. Just come this way."

As they followed her out of the hall, Lewis stiffened with horror. If they went into the library, the
first thing they'd clap eyes on would be the *Mona
Lisa!* And although Casimir had told him that no
one would give it a second glance, he was not so
sure. The police weren't fools and he just couldn't
take the risk.

Thanking his lucky stars that he hadn't made
a wish yet, he rushed to the bathroom mirror, his
eyes full of alarm. A hundred thoughts raced in a
jumbled torrent through his mind. What if they
searched the house? They would find all his treasures! They'd call him a thief and he'd go to prison!
And what would his mum and dad say?

"I wish," he hurriedly said to Casimir, "I wish
that you'd send back all the things I've wished
for from that book, send them back to where they
came from! Please! Right now!"

He crossed his fingers tightly as he made his
way through to his bedroom and paused at the
door, scared that nothing would have happened;
that they'd all still be there. He looked anxiously
round and saw to his relief that the room was bare.
They'd gone! Thank goodness, they had all gone!

He fell on the bed, trembling with shock and
relief. He could hardly believe the narrow escape
he'd had. But niggling in the back of his mind was
the knowledge that he still had to make a wish
every day. Casimir was being awkward making
things more and more difficult. Now he was saying
that he couldn't wish for anything made of wood
because he'd already wished for shelves to put his
treasures on. He couldn't wish for ivory because of

the statue and he couldn't wish for food because he'd once asked for a Chinese meal. He curled up in a ball and hugged his knees. If only, *if only* he could get rid of Casimir!

His thoughts went round and round in circles as he tried to think of something that Casimir couldn't do. He knew him well enough now to believe that he actually could do everything. Even moving Mount Everest wasn't an option as he'd probably cause an earthquake to swallow it and then push it up somewhere else. He'd never felt so depressed in his life.

Lewis only ventured downstairs because he was feeling hungry. His attitude to Mrs Sinclair had long since changed as, despite her prim appearance, he had soon discovered that she was a wonderful cook. "Are there any of those biscuits left that you made yesterday, Mrs Sinclair," he asked, peering hopefully round the kitchen door.

She eyed him shrewdly. What was the matter with him? He looked really pale and ill-looking. She hoped he wasn't coming down with something. "Yes, there are still some left," she said, feeling quite sorry for him as she took the biscuit tin from a shelf. "How many would you like?"

"Five or six," he hazarded. "I'm starving!"

She counted them. "There are eight left," she said. "If you have five today there'll still be three left over. Or you could divide them equally … four now and four later?"

Her words took Lewis right back to his primary school and his teacher saying in a tone of exasperation. "It's impossible, Lewis! You can't do it! You can't possibly make three lots of five out of twelve counters. You can only make two lots with two left over!"

"That's it!" he said, in sudden wonder. *"That's it!"*

"What's what?" asked a startled Mrs Sinclair as he hugged her and started to laugh. "Mrs Sinclair, you're totally fab!"

"Well, now," she said, pleased despite herself, "you just calm down and I'll get you a drink. What's it to be?"

"Irn Bru, please," he grinned as he waltzed round the kitchen, eyes alight with excitement.

Casimir stirred uneasily inside him. He couldn't read Lewis's thoughts but he could sense his moods, and for the life of him he couldn't figure out why he was suddenly so blazingly happy. Perhaps, he thought, it was because all the treasures had gone back to their rightful owners and the police couldn't charge him with anything. Not, he thought, that the police would ever have found out, but Lewis, for all his weird ideas, was turning out to be surprisingly law-abiding.

Needless to say, the news that night was full of it! The sudden, mystifying return of the *Mona Lisa,* to say nothing of all the other stolen items, was headline news on all the channels and as reporters revelled in the mystery, the speculation looked like lasting for days to come. Lewis, however, had almost forgotten the return of the *Mona Lisa* in his anxiety to get the better of Casimir.

"We had a bargain, Casimir," Lewis reminded him when he'd finished watching the news and gone upstairs to his room. "I seem to remember you saying that if I gave you a task that you couldn't do, then you would be *my* slave and *your* magic would be *mine?*"

Casimir nodded from the mirror and watched sourly as Lewis emptied a box of chocolates onto his desk and counted them.

"This is the test?" Casimir said in surprise. "A test with chocolates?"

Lewis nodded. "There are eleven chocolates on the desk," he said. "I want you to make them into four sets of three. Now go ahead and do it!"

Casimir's eyes rounded in amazement. Such a simple test but he knew just by looking at them that there was no way he could make four sets of three out of eleven chocolates. He didn't even bother to try and his face was set in lines of absolute disbelief as he was forced to concede defeat.

"I can't do it!" he admitted, totally stunned at the turn of events.

"Right!" said Lewis triumphantly. "Now you are my slave and your magic is mine! Agreed?"

Casimir didn't answer and, looking at him apprehensively, Lewis was suddenly assailed by doubt. Rather than keep the bargain, Casimir might just turn him into a toad or a frog or whatever magicians did when they were cornered. In actual fact, he needn't have worried, however, for Casimir was not only a very grand magician but also a prince. It would never have entered his head to renege on the agreement they had made.

"Yes," muttered Casimir, looking suddenly very

old indeed. "Yes, that is the case. There is, however, one thing, Master. One favour I'd like to ask you."

"What's that?" Lewis asked suspiciously.

"It's about my son, Prince Kalman."

"What about Prince Kalman?" Lewis asked.

"The goblin said Kalman was trapped in a magic mirror that was set for Edinburgh. That means that somewhere in Edinburgh there must be a mirror that holds my son prisoner."

"But there are thousands of mirrors in Edinburgh!" Lewis frowned. "How on earth will you recognize it?"

"Magic mirrors are special mirrors, Master. They are at least seven feet tall and have iron frames decorated with beasts, birds and flowers."

"Well, that ought to be easy enough to spot," Lewis said interestedly. "But why do you have to look for it? Can't you just magic it here like you did your carpet?"

"Magic mirrors have two halves, Master. That is how they work. They have to be set so that they connect. If you walk through a mirror in Edinburgh you can step out of it anywhere in the world, depending on the setting. But if one half disintegrates the connection is broken and you can't magic up half a mirror. It has to be found. So, if by any chance I ever see a magic mirror, can I bring it to your notice, Master? And ask you to release my son?"

"I'll do that on one condition, Casimir," Lewis said. "If I release your son from the magic mirror, I want you both out of my life completely. Agreed?"

"Agreed," nodded Casimir. "Thank you, Master."

And with that, his face disappeared from the little hand mirror.

Lewis started in surprise as, for the first time in weeks, he saw his own reflection appear instead. Full of sudden hope, he got up and ran first to his dressing table, and then to the mirror in the bathroom just to make sure Casimir had really gone — and gave a heartfelt sigh of relief as his own reflection stared back at him.

13. The Black Shadow

Next morning, Lewis closed the last of his exercise books, put his pencils in his pencil case and pushed the neat pile of homework to one side with a sigh of relief. Thank goodness that was finished, he thought, looking at his watch. He'd timed it nicely; it was just about lunchtime. His spirits lightened as he went downstairs to the kitchen for Mrs Sinclair had promised to make him a chicken curry and the smell was drifting tantalizingly through the house.

As he pushed open the door, he saw that the small kitchen television set was on and from the sound of the commentator's voice, there was yet another disaster taking place somewhere in the world.

"There's been a terrible accident on the Forth Bridge, Lewis," Mrs Sinclair said. She was stirring the curry but her eyes never left the screen.

Lewis gasped. "That's near here, isn't it?" he said, looking at its distinctive shape. He'd seen pictures of it and knew it lay close to Edinburgh.

"Aye. Two trains collided and half of one train is hanging off the bridge. The carriages are full of people and they're scared that the whole train might slip down into the water with them all in it!"

"Gosh! That's awful!"

"Here," she said, spooning a generous helping of

curry over a gleaming mound of white rice, "have your lunch at the kitchen table and you'll be able to see what's happening."

Lewis ate the curry absent-mindedly, his eyes fixed on the TV screen. It was really quite frightening. Even the commentator was affected as stumbling groups of passengers were led along the tracks from the wrecked trains. Lewis could hear the tremble in his voice as he described the rescue attempts that were being set up to try to get people out of the carriages that had slipped off the bridge. It was going to be a dangerous operation as the whole train was balanced so precariously that the slightest jerk might send it toppling into the water. Helicopters were of no use as they couldn't operate so close to the bridge. All in all, he didn't seem too confident of the outcome.

"Oh, my goodness," Mrs Sinclair jumped up as part of the train hanging crazily from the bridge gave a dreadful lurch. They could hear the people in the carriages screaming. "How on earth are they ever going to rescue them?" she said, twisting her hands.

"I ..." he searched his mind for a reason, "I can't watch," he said. "It's too frightening. I'm going out, Mrs Sinclair." And he pushed his plate to one side and dashed up the stairs to his room.

"Casimir!" he snapped at the bathroom mirror. "Show yourself to me."

Casimir appeared. "Casimir, did you see what was happening on the television downstairs?"

"Yes, of course, Master."

"Listen, There's no way that anybody can save

the people on that train. The two end carriages
are hanging over the water and if anybody tries to
climb out they'll send the whole lot crashing into
the Forth. Can you save them by magic? Or something?" he asked hopefully.

Casimir looked at Lewis consideringly and
sighed. After hundreds of years imprisoned in
the well at Al Antara, he thought sourly, it had to
be a do-gooder like Lewis who had released him!
Still, he mused, rescuing the people on the train
might do much to relieve the crashing boredom
of the schoolboy's totally uneventful life. He bent
his mind to the task and instantly came up with
a solution — for he had, as it happened, quite
enjoyed reading Lewis's comics with him. "What
if I were to turn you into Superman or even the
Black Shadow?" he offered. "The Shadow, I think,
would be more suitable as you're so young. How
about it? All in black, wearing a mask and a cloak
with stars on it?"

Lewis sat up straight, his eyes suddenly shining.
"What a fantastic idea, Casimir," he gasped. "The
Black Shadow! But … can you really make me fly?"

Casimir looked at him exasperatedly. "Of course
I can," he said shortly. "I'd hardly have suggested
it otherwise, would I?"

And, in an instant, Lewis changed completely.
He looked in the mirror. There he stood, looking
slightly taller than normal, but the spitting image
of the Black Shadow.

He swirled his cloak experimentally before
pressing down on the soles of his feet to see if
he could really fly. Excitement gripped him as he

lifted gently off the carpet and soared into the air.

"Use your arms to change direction," Casimir recommended hastily as Lewis, cloak flapping, headed straight for a solid-looking wardrobe.

"This is great, Casimir," he said, changing direction and ducking frantically as he almost hit the light shade. Landing beside the window, he pulled it up so that he could scramble out onto the sill and, trying to ignore the drop to the street, took a deep breath.

"I think you'd better make me invisible until I get to the bridge," he suggested as he launched himself into space from the windowsill. It was the hardest thing Lewis had ever done in his life and he gulped in relief as his cloak spread out behind him as he sailed through the air. Stretching his arms in front of him, he found that he could guide his flight and, soaring upwards to get his bearings, immediately saw the dim outline of the Forth Bridge in the distance.

The air was freezing and whistled past him as he flew. "Casimir! I'm frozen!" he yelled. "Doesn't this outfit have central heating?" Casimir obviously obliged as a wave of heat shimmered through the black suit and he relaxed gratefully as it warmed him through.

The news commentator choked into his microphone and did a double-take as the black, cloaked figure suddenly appeared out of nowhere and flew over the waters of the Forth, heading for the huge criss-crossed spars of the bridge.

"What on earth!" he stammered. "I don't believe it …"

And as each and every camera swung round to follow his flight, Lewis swooped down to land on one of the great girders. Now that he had actually arrived on the scene, he suddenly felt very scared. Conscious that every eye was on him, he worried that he might make a mess of the whole thing. The bridge, for a start, was no longer the tiny meccano-like structure it had seemed on the television set. It was immense! Even the train seemed three times the size of normal trains, its tilted underside hung with row upon row of wheels like some enormous caterpillar.

"Hey, you!" a policeman shouted, running up the railway line. "Get down from there at once!"

Lewis looked at him through the slits in his mask. "I've come to get these people out of the carriages," he shouted back.

"Don't be a fool!" the policeman yelled. "Get down from there at once!" Lewis ignored him and, before the policeman could get near enough to catch him, pushed himself off the girder and swooped to hover beside the dangling carriages. The people inside were as still as statues. Nobody needed to tell them what would happen if they made any sudden movement. They followed Lewis with their eyes and a woman started to sob.

"This is absolutely unbelievable," the commentator said excitedly. "We have some kind of Superman here. He's hovering just above the stricken carriages ..."

Lewis scanned the train. Many of the windows had fallen out and he decided to try to lift people through them. Fervently hoping that Casimir had given him the strength of at least ten men, he hovered above one window and reached inside.

"Hold your hands up and I'll pull you clear," he said to a young girl. "Just relax. And you be ready next," he said to the woman beside her.

A cheer rang out from the bridge as he soared upwards holding the girl by the arms and passed her into the care of a waiting ambulance crew.

As he swooped back to the train, an engineer ran up the track. The cameras zoomed in on him as he stopped by the television news crew.

The engineer was distraught. "Get off the bridge, quickly!" he said urgently. "The main bolts have snapped and the carriages are hanging only on a few links. They won't be able to hold it for long! Get off the bridge at once!"

"Clear the bridge! Clear the bridge!" The order drifted down to Lewis as he swung upwards with a mother and her baby.

The ambulance crew stayed, however, the medics taking it in turns to carry the stretchers back to the ambulances as Lewis deposited more and more people by the side of the tracks.

A little group of engineers stood watching at the end of the bridge; white faced, grim and staring. They, alone, of all the watchers, knew the weakness of the pitifully few links that held the carriages to the rest of the train and waited in despair for the inevitable crack that would signal the breaking of the last few bolts. The television commentator who had thought of asking one of them to come across and give his opinion in front of the cameras, took one look at their faces and decided against it.

In the end, Lewis had to force himself to go inside the carriages to reach people, especially those that had been injured. The strength Casimir had given him made it easy for him to lift them but knowing that the whole set up might collapse at any minute, made it an absolutely hair-raising task. He'd have been even more concerned had he known just how much magic Casimir was using to keep the dangling carriages attached to the rest of the train and it was only when Lewis carried the last man from the last carriage that Casimir cut the spell. The bolts then did what they should have done at least half an hour previously. They snapped with a vicious crack — and with a tearing, grinding jerk, the carriages toppled slowly from the bridge and fell into the dull, grey waters of the Firth of Forth.

Everyone was so busy watching the carriages fall into the water that Lewis was able to become invisible again without anyone noticing. He was utterly exhausted and rested for a while on one of the girders before heading once again for Edinburgh.

"My, you missed such a thrilling rescue!" Mrs Sinclair said as he came in. "You should have stayed and watched it, Lewis! It was just like the cinema. They're calling him the Shadow, like some comic-strip character. He rescued everybody out of that train, you know! It was wonderful!"

"The Shadow?" Lewis pretended to be surprised. "You're having me on!" he exclaimed. "He's a character in my comic books!"

"Aye, but this was a real person, all dressed up in a mask and a cloak. He could fly through the air, just like Superman. And he rescued so many people! Wonderful, he was!"

"I wish I'd seen him," Lewis did his best to sound disconsolate. "Do you think they'll show it again?"

"Ocht, of course they will. It'll be repeated all night, I should think," Mrs Sinclair said, "but it'll no' be as thrilling as watching it when it was happening! What they can't understand is how the carriages didn't fall sooner. The engineers were saying they were only held up by a few links!"

"Were they really?" Lewis said slowly.

"You owe me, Lewis!" Casimir said softly as Mrs Sinclair went to serve the dinner. "You owe me big time, believe me!"

14. The Shadow Strikes Again

"I bet it's him," Neil muttered to Clara as they sat glued to the television, watching as the black, cloaked figure carried passenger after passenger out of the wrecked carriages that dangled so perilously from the Forth Bridge.

"Bet it's who?" asked the Ranger, looking at Neil in surprise.

"The boy that Kitor saw on Arthur's Seat," Neil answered.

"So?" Clara didn't sound convinced.

"It must be! Who else is there in Edinburgh that has the magic to do stuff like that?"

"We don't really know a lot about the world of magic," his father said doubtfully. "Perhaps there are other magicians in Scotland that we haven't heard about."

Kitor flapped his wings. "The MacArthurs are the only magic people here," he said. "I don't know where this boy has come from but he is definitely a magician and a powerful magician at that. The magic shield the MacArthurs put round Arthur's Seat wouldn't have kept him out otherwise."

"I wish the MacArthurs would come back," Janet MacLean sighed. "Is there no way we could get in touch with them, John?"

"No way at all," her husband replied. "We'll just have to wait until they turn up!"

"We know where the boy lives," Neil said, looking at his father doubtfully. "Kitor still keeps an eye on the house. If he could let us know when he goes out, we might be able to follow him."

"No, Neil," Mrs MacLean said firmly, "if he's as powerful a magician as Kitor says, then it might be dangerous. Let's wait and see what the MacArthurs have to say when they get back."

"Your mother's quite right, Neil," pointed out their father, "for if he was trying to get into the hill to see the MacArthur then it follows that they must know one another. And I can't help feeling that the MacArthur might not like us interfering in his affairs."

"That's true, Dad," Clara said, nodding thoughtfully. "I hadn't thought of it like that."

"I'd just concentrate on the pantomime, if I were you, and leave the MacArthurs to sort out the Shadow when they get back."

Neil and Clara looked at one another and nodded agreement, their minds already elsewhere. For the basement and cellars of the Assembly Hall were now stacked with scenery and props for the pantomime and during the rehearsal that night, they planned to search for the entrance to the Underground City.

Lewis, too, was watching television that evening, clicking the remote control and moving from channel to channel. Every station was full of it. The Shadow was going to be headline news in all of tomorrow's newspapers!

"Casimir," he said when he was up in his room

getting ready for bed. "Can you tell when accidents and things happen?"

"When they happen, yes," was the answer. "Nobody can see an accident *before* it happens, Lewis."

"Will you tell me when anything happens; you know, like it did today? I can't help thinking that if I hadn't become the Shadow then the people I rescued would all be dead now. It's a scary thought, Casimir."

Casimir quite liked the idea and cheered up considerably at the thought of some action. He'd never, of course, have said anything to Lewis but quite frankly found living inside him a dead bore. "There are a couple of climbers stuck in the Cuillins, if you're interested," he said casually. "The rescue services can't get near them. It's blowing a blizzard over there and their helicopters are grounded. They'll both be dead before morning."

"Over where, exactly?" asked Lewis, whose geography wasn't very good.

"The Cuillins are mountains on the Isle of Skye, off the west coast," Casimir said. "Really, Lewis! If you spent as much time on your schoolwork as you do reading those comics, you'd be a lot better informed!"

"I'm really tired, Casimir," Lewis said, looking longingly at his bed.

"You don't have to go," Casimir said. "Pretend I didn't tell you."

"But you did and if I don't go, they'll die! Can you see them, Casimir?"

Casimir flashed a picture into Lewis's mind.

Two climbers huddled together on a narrow ledge in the middle of a snowstorm.

"Let's go, Casimir," Lewis said quietly. "There's no way I can leave them. They look as though they're going to fall at any minute."

"We'll travel fast, Master," Casimir promised.

He was as good as his word. Lewis swung out of his window and as he soared over George Street, seemed to go into overdrive. The sudden burst of speed shot him like a rocket over the castle and the rest of the city at a terrific rate that at first took his breath away. He soon became accustomed to it, however, and watched as the landscape rolled under him like a moving carpet; as though it was he who was stationary and the country that moved beneath him. It was only when they hit the fringes of the blizzard that Casimir slowed the pace.

Lewis had never been to the west coast of Scotland and although they were only vague, shadowy shapes seen through the driving snow, the mountains towered around him; strange, threatening and overwhelming in their presence. He felt like an alien as Casimir navigated him towards the ledge on which the climbers huddled, already half-frozen by the biting cold.

Their eyes rounded in terror as he approached them, black and evil-looking, out of the blizzard. There was no place to turn; all they could do was press themselves back against the solid bulk of the mountain and hope that their end would be swift. The masked face, the black cloak and the fact that he was flying in the air over a drop of thousands of feet convinced them that if he wasn't the devil himself, he was certainly the next best thing.

"Calm them down, Casimir," Lewis whispered under his breath. "I'll never get anywhere near them otherwise!"

Magic rayed down on them from the cloaked figure and Lewis watched as their fear faded, and it was only when hope stirred in their eyes that he landed on the ledge beside them.

"Hi!" he said casually.

It was probably the best thing he could have said. James and Charles, both students at Edinburgh University, were bright lads and, as they instinctively doubted that devils in any shape or form opened conversations with "Hi," they looked at one another in relief and waited for more.

Lewis was actually feeling more than a bit embarrassed. What on earth was he going to say? I'm the Shadow? I've come to rescue you? Both sounded totally over the top.

"Who on earth are you?" James asked, his lips barely able to move for the snow crusting his face.

"Never mind who I am," Lewis said hurriedly. "Let's get you out of here. Don't worry, I can carry you both," he added as they looked at him in amazement.

"How do you propose to do that?" James queried. Charles, who was drifting in and out of consciousness, didn't say anything and James, after a quick glance, held on to him tighter.

"Let's warm them up!" Lewis said quietly.

Casimir took the hint and again a ray of magic

enveloped the two climbers who relaxed as a delicious feeling of warmth stole over them, Charles stirred and James's eyes mirrored his relief. Who or what this strange creature was, he didn't know but as the grim prospect of certain death started to fade from his mind, he found himself hoping wildly that perhaps, just perhaps, they might come out of this in one piece.

"Take Charles first," he said hoarsely. "He's in a bad way. There ought to be a Mountain Rescue team in the area. They'd have called it out when we didn't get back to the hotel!"

Lewis hovered in the air and settled himself beside Charles, pulling his arms over his shoulders and hoisting him on his back. After the Forth Bridge affair there wasn't much he didn't know about lifting and carrying.

"Any sign of a Mountain Rescue team, Casimir?" he asked as they dropped towards the valley below.

"You're homed in on it," was Casimir's reply.

And sure enough, the bent, plodding figures of the Mountain Rescue Team, battling against the force of the blizzard, soon loomed up through the snow.

The leader of the team threw out an arm to signal a halt as, out of the whirling flakes, a strange, black-caped figure swooped to land beside them. Lewis grinned slightly at their astounded faces and knew that before long his sudden appearance would be the talk of the Highlands and Islands. "Is one of you a doctor?" he asked, heaving Charles off his shoulders. Two men immediately moved forward while others, seeing the slumped figure of the climber, opened their packs and started assembling a stretcher.

"You'll need two stretchers," he told them. "If you just hang on, I'll bring the other one."

"He's falling!" Casimir interrupted him abruptly and at the same time whirled Lewis into the air and up the sheer side of the mountain to where a hooded, bulky figure tumbled head over heels through the whirling snowflakes; James, who had tried to shift to a more comfortable position when Lewis had taken Charles from his grasp, had moved awkwardly, lost his balance and toppled from the ledge. He could hardly believe his luck when two arms, as strong as steel, grasped him firmly in mid-air. "Relax," a boyish voice said, "you're safe now!"

"I ... don't know who, or what, you are," James whispered. "But thanks all the same. I'd be a goner without you!"

Lewis grinned and Casimir, who, in the past, had rarely gone out of his way to help anyone, was again visited by that strange feeling of elation that he couldn't quite put a name to — but one thing he *did* know was that this Shadow business was just what he needed to add a bit of spice to Lewis's totally uninteresting life. Nevertheless, the boy's knowledge of geography — and history, for that matter, was quite deplorable. Lewis, Casimir decided, was going to have to develop the urge to read and learn; for he, himself, was anxious to know what had gone on in the world during the hundreds of years that he'd spent cooped up in the well at Al Antara and the Robinson's library, he decided, was the ideal place to find out.

15. Lost in the Underground City

Clara shivered as she looked around. This part of the Underground City was definitely scary. It was nothing like Mary King's Close which, she now realized, must have been extensively renovated to make it fit for tourists to visit. Its neat, white-washed walls certainly bore no resemblance to the filthy jumble of dark, narrow alleys under the Assembly Hall. The houses here were derelict and their black, empty windows seemed to watch them as they crept fearfully past.

"We'll have to be careful not to get lost," she said worriedly, as Neil's torch lit up the old, dusty streets.

Neil, however, hardly heard her. He was fascinated. "What a place," he breathed. "Just think, Clara, no one's probably walked down this street for hundreds of years!" He shone his torch through the windows of some of the houses and peered in, but the rooms were empty.

"Let's have a look inside this one!" he said excitedly, climbing the few steps to its gaping doorway. "You never know, we might find something really old and interesting inside." Clara didn't think so but followed him in nervously, picking her way over broken floors and nudging scattered heaps of crumbling debris with the toes of her trainers. The old house was a rabbit-warren of small rooms and passages and to this day Clara reckons that they left it by a different door from the one they went in by. The narrow streets all looked much the same and it was only when they turned to go back to the cellars of the Assembly Hall that they found that they couldn't find their way. They wandered up and down until, with sinking hearts, realized that they were well and truly lost.

"I don't believe this!" Neil said. "We can't be lost! I'm sure we came along this street! The stair that leads up to the cellars should be about here!"

"Well, it isn't," Clara said in a small voice. "I think we got lost in that house. We must have left by the back door and ended up in another alley."

"Let's go back along and see if we can find it again, then," Neil said, trying to sound cheerful.

"Couldn't we call our carpets?" Clara asked hopefully.

Neil shook his head. "They wouldn't be able to get in," he pointed out. "Mary King's Close is locked for the night and we shut the basement door behind us when we came down here, remember?"

"We should have brought chalk with us so that we could mark our path," Clara groaned, wishing that she'd thought of it before. "You know, like Hansel and Gretel." But although they looked at each house carefully, they didn't recognize the house they'd been in and soon afterwards found themselves close to a totally unfamiliar street that sloped steeply downwards.

"Look," said Neil, striding forward, "this must be where the bank robbers hang out. They've been here and not long ago either," he said, picking up a chipped saucer that stood on a pile of old crates. It was full of cigarette-ends. His nose wrinkled in disgust as the smell drifted round him. "One of the crooks must smoke!" he muttered, replacing the ashtray hurriedly. The heavy smoker was, of course, Wullie who couldn't last for more than fifteen minutes without a fag. He reeked of cigarette smoke and then wondered why the non-smokers in the pub, edged to the other end of the bar!

Clara looked round nervously. "And this must be where they're working," she said, shining her torch on a scatter of tools, propped against the wall. "Look, they've got a lantern as well."

"Now that we're here, we should go down and see how far they've got," Neil said slowly, letting the light of the torch shine down the dark, threatening curve of the alley. "I wonder if they've reached the bank yet."

"It looks dead creepy, doesn't it," Clara said doubtfully, not at all anxious to venture further.

Neil shivered. "Come on," he said grimly, "we'd better get it over with! I'll borrow their lantern so that we have a bit more light. Careful how you go though; there are still bits of brick and stuff lying around."

Murdo and Wullie had obviously been busy, for the alleyway was more or less clear of rubble. When they were about half way down, Clara tripped and fell over a jagged brick. She cried out as she hit the ground. "I've torn my jeans and I think I've cut my knee," she muttered, getting to her feet and wiping her hands on the side of her jacket, "*and* grazed my hands!"

"For Pete's sake, Clara! You'll be fine!" Neil muttered as Clara dabbed at her cut knee and hobbled after him.

"Look, Neil," she said in relief, "this must be what they were looking for." Neil lifted the lantern as they walked up to a very new-looking red-brick wall. A pick and a shovel lay propped against it.

"The bank!" Neil said in triumph. "This wall must have been built by the bank! Bet you the vaults are behind it!"

Clara looked at the pick and the shovel and nodded. "I reckon they're ready to break in," she said.

"Yeah," agreed her brother, holding up the lantern, "and," he said, his eyes searching the alley, "it doesn't look as though they've damaged any of the houses, either. The Plague People must still be holed up in their cellars."

"Great!" Clara said sarcastically. "Thanks for that!" She looked round nervously, horrified at the thought that, had the crooks been careless, they might actually have come face to face with the Plague People.

"It'll cheer up Mary King, no end," Neil continued. "She was really worried that they'd let them escape."

Clara shivered at the thought. "Come on, Neil," she urged, "let's go back now. We've seen enough, haven't we?"

Clara was panting as she climbed up the steep hill to the top of the alley. Going up, she decided, was almost as bad as going down! "Get a move on, Neil," she gasped. "We've got to find our way out of here!"

"Have you then?" said a rough voice as the beam of a powerful torch shone on them.

"They're just a couple of kids, Murdo," Wullie said in relief, peering out from behind him. "Just a couple of kids!"

"What are you doing down here?" Murdo said grimly, taking in Clara's torn jeans and grimy face.

Real tears of relief came to Clara's eyes as she saw the two men. "Oh, thank goodness," she said, the tears spilling down her cheeks. "I … I thought we were going to be shut in here forever!"

"We were exploring the cellars in the Assembly Hall," Neil explained, "and we got lost in all those old passageways."

"We're so glad to see you," Clara smiled, wiping the tears from her eyes, totally unaware that she was leaving black streaks across her face. "Can you show us the way out? Please!"

"Where did you say you came from?" asked Murdo.

"The Assembly Hall," Neil said. "We're in the pantomime."

"Pantomime, eh!" Murdo said thoughtfully, with a glance at Wullie. "Now what pantomime would that be?"

"Ali Baba and … and the Forty Thieves," Clara said. She saw the funny side of her words the minute she'd said them and stuck her nails sharply into the palms of her hands so that she wouldn't giggle.

Wullie, however, let out a real roar of laughter and even Murdo smiled sardonically. Neil and

Clara eyed one another warily and managed to look puzzled as they joined in.

"*Ali Baba,* eh!" Murdo said. "Well, well! And when is it on?"

"The dress rehearsal is in a few days time," Neil said slowly, wondering at his interest, "and it opens on Monday of next week."

"Monday, eh," Murdo repeated thoughtfully.

"It's really good," Clara said, smiling shyly at Wullie. "Matt Lafferty's in it. You know ... the guy who won that TV show? He's fabulous!"

"Matt Lafferty," Wullie grinned amiably. "Aye, I read that he was in a panto this year. He's a great guy, he is!"

Murdo, meanwhile, got his map out of his pocket and spread it on their makeshift table. "Where did you say you came from?" he asked. "The Assembly Hall, wasn't it?"

Neil nodded, fascinated at the sight of the map. "There's the Mound," he said, following its curve down towards Princes Street, "and the Assembly Hall must be above those streets there, don't you think?"

"Aye," Murdo agreed. "Now we're about here so we'll have to take this road that curves slightly."

"Could you take us?" asked Clara shyly. "We've been so frightened and I don't want to get lost again!"

"No problem," Murdo said with a friendliness that left Wullie gawping. "We'll take you there and see you safely back with your friends. Don't worry!"

Neil looked guilty. "The thing is," he said, "we didn't tell anyone that we were going to explore down here and … well, we don't want to get into trouble."

"Yes," added Clara, "if we're caught, they mightn't let us be in the pantomime any more."

"You'll no' be caught, lassie," Wullie growled. "We're no' going to shop you!"

"That works both ways, though," Murdo said, looking at Neil meaningfully. *"We* don't shop *you — you* don't shop *us?* Okay?"

Neil looked at him and read the menace in his eyes. "Okay," he agreed, his voice suddenly sounding shaky.

Clara looked at him sharply. What on earth was the matter with Neil?

Neil looked at her and shook his head slightly. He had been just about to warn the robbers about the Plague People as Mary King had said but the look in Murdo's eyes had stopped him short. He felt a sick feeling in the pit of his stomach as it suddenly dawned on him that if he gave him the ghosts' warning, then Murdo would realize that they knew of his plans to rob the bank.

Not a good idea, thought Neil, his mind racing. It had been a big mistake to tell them that nobody knew where they were. Still, he reasoned, they'd got as far as the bank without letting the Plague People out, so maybe it wouldn't matter if he didn't pass on the message.

Convinced by the look on Neil's face that he wouldn't say a word to anyone about them being in the Underground City, Murdo relaxed. "Great!" he said, sounding a lot friendlier. "Now, let's get you back to the Assembly Hall!"

Clara sighed with relief as they reached the shabby door that led to the cellars of the Assembly Hall and grinned at Neil who still looked rather white. Thank goodness they'd got back safely, he thought, as he thanked Murdo and Wullie and, with a brief wave of his hand, followed Clara who, hoping they hadn't been missed, was already clattering her way up the narrow flight of stairs to rejoin the rehearsal.

The crooks watched them go but as Wullie turned to go back the way they'd come, Murdo held him back. "Hang on, Wullie," he muttered. "What say you that we go up and have a nose about?"

Wullie puffed slightly as they climbed the stairs but once backstage they moved purposefully and as no one thought to question whether they belonged to the King's or were Assembly Hall staff, they were able to make quite a thorough reconnaissance of the place.

"Got some plasticine on you then, Wullie?" queried Murdo.

"Never travel without it," Wullie grinned, fishing around in one of the many inner pockets that had been specially built into his capacious overcoat. He knew perfectly well what was required of him for he, too, had noticed that the caretaker had left the keys in the basement doors. It took seconds for Wullie to take them out and press them gently, but deeply, into the plasticene.

"You're no' thinking of nicking any this stuff, are you?" he asked, nodding at the prop table as he carefully stashed the imprints of the keys in his coat. Eyes gleaming, he picked up an Aladdin's lamp and looked speculatively over the piles of brightly-coloured fake jewels and the glitter of gold-painted mirrors, vases, lamps and trays that lay strewn across the props table.

Murdo looked at Wullie and almost sighed. "No, Wullie," he said, "no, the keys are not for that!" He shook his head. "Get real, will you! What would I be doing with this load of tat, you idiot?"

"What do you want the keys for then?" mumbled Wullie, fascinated by the exotic glitter of the props.

"When we've lifted the cash from the bank we can hardly walk out through Deacon Brodie's Tavern with the loot, can we?"

Wullie looked thoughtful and Murdo persevered. "Even that load of thick-heads will suspect something if we walk through the pub carrying hefty sacks of money, don't you think?"

Wullie looked at him in sudden understanding.

"Especially," continued Murdo, "if they've heard the explosion when we blow up the vault! And they probably will hear it. The pub's no' that far away!"

Wullie nodded.

"But," Murdo went on cunningly, "they'll no' hear the noise from away up here, will they?"

Wullie shook his head.

"So we can bring the sacks of cash up here …"

"And," said Wullie, his brain working at last, "make our get-away through these cellars instead!"

"You've got it in one!" Murdo grinned, clapping him on the back. "We'll have the keys cut tomorrow!"

16. Chasing Shadows

Margaret Grant looked at her husband across the breakfast table as Lewis got up and muttered something about just going to do a bit of work in the library.

"Did you say anything to him, Bob?" she asked her husband.

"About what?" her husband enquired, lowering the newspaper.

"Well, he seems to spend most of his time reading these days and I thought you might have been ... pushing him to do a bit of work."

Bob Grant shook his head. "I haven't said a word to Lewis but I'm glad to see him taking an interest in something other than comics!"

"But the books he's reading, Bob. Huge volumes on Scottish History ..."

Her husband looked puzzled. "That's certainly a big jump from comics," he said, thoughtfully. "Good for him! Heriot's is certainly having a positive influence on him."

"He was talking about Rizzio's murder the other day. He knew all about it, you know. To hear him speak, you'd have thought he'd seen it happen!"

"I didn't read about that," her husband turned the pages of his newspaper.

Margaret Grant raised her eyebrows. "For goodness sake, Bob, *David* Rizzio! In Holyrood Palace. In the days of Mary, Queen of Scots!"

"Oh! *That* David Rizzio," he muttered. "Sorry, I wasn't with you. I've been reading all about this Shadow chap that seems to be doing the work of half the police forces in Scotland! He rescued some children from a burning building last night."

"He's become quite a hero," Margaret Grant smiled. "A lot of people owe him their lives."

"Nevertheless, I think Sir Archibald Thompson must be getting slightly worried," her husband said, folding his newspaper.

"Who's he?" asked his wife.

"Sir Archie is the Chief Constable of Edinburgh," her husband replied, "and by my reckoning, this business must be giving him quite a few sleepless nights!"

"Over the Shadow, you mean? But the Shadow is doing the country a service, Bob! Look at the lives he's saving!"

"Superman only exists in comics, Margaret, and it isn't really a matter of who this chap is, it's *what* he is that matters! That's what must be worrying Sir Archie!"

Bob Grant was quite right. The Chief Constable *was* worried and, realizing at once that the world of magic must be involved somewhere along the line, fervently wished that the MacArthurs would hurry up and come back from Turkey. At that particular moment, he'd have quite happily given up his pension for a peek into the MacArthur's crystal ball!

The only thing he was really sure about was that the Shadow was a boy. The climbers, the policeman on the bridge and the train survivors had all said he was a young lad. And as the only young lad that Sir Archie knew who was connected to the world of magic was Neil MacLean, he voiced his suspicions to Sir James.

"Neil MacLean! The Shadow!" Sir James had sounded stunned. "Well, he could be, I suppose, but I doubt it. In fact," he paused, counting back the days, "I'm sure he isn't. I was on my way to the distillery the day of the train crash and saw I saw Neil and Clara at the foot of the High Street near the Palace."

"Thank goodness, for that," Archie Thompson sank back in his chair with a sigh of relief. "I didn't really think so but what other young lad is there in Edinburgh that has anything to do with magic and magicians?"

"The Shadow might not live in Edinburgh," Sir James pointed out. "He's been rescuing people here, there and everywhere as far as I can gather. Mind you, if it's the low-down on the world of magic you're after, you could always ask Kitor," he suggested.

"That's an idea," the Chief Constable's voice brightened at the thought.

"He once belonged to Prince Kalman, remember," added Sir James, "so, he must know a lot about what goes on. There are probably wizards and magicians round the place that we've never heard of."

"That's true," the Chief Constable nodded. "Er ... could we meet at the MacLean's cottage, do you think, James? It's more informal and ... well, I can hardly question a crow here at HQ without causing a sensation!"

"Actually, I'm going to the cottage this afternoon. I'll be there just after three. The MacLeans are quite involved in the pantomime, you know. Janet's been working backstage, ironing all the costumes, and the Ranger's made a lot of papier mâché food for the banqueting scene ... that sort of thing. Why don't you give Janet a ring? I'm sure she'd love to see you and I bet they've got all sorts of theories about the Shadow!"

That afternoon, as the Chief Constable relaxed by the fire in the MacLean's living room, nursing a cup of coffee, he brought up the subject. "I've really come to pick your brains about the Shadow," he admitted with a smile, "to see if you have any ideas."

There was an awkward silence as the MacLeans looked at one another doubtfully. Archie Thompson sipped his coffee and shot a keen glance at Sir James. Surely it wasn't Neil after all?

"The thing is," said the Ranger apologetically, "we know who the Shadow is."

The Chief Constable spluttered into his coffee and Mrs MacLean reached for a box of tissues.

"You *know* who the Shadow is?" he repeated, mopping coffee from his uniform.

The Ranger nodded. "Yes," he said. "We *think* we know. I can't think why I didn't tell you about it! How stupid of me!"

"Who is he, then? Is it someone you know? A friend of Neil's, maybe?"

The Ranger shook his head. "No, nothing like

that. The boy's a complete stranger. Actually, it was Kitor who saw him," he said, nodding to where Kitor perched on Clara's shoulder. "Apparently, the MacArthurs left a protective barrier round the hill when they left. Kitor says it only keeps out magicians and the like and ... well, when he was out on the hill, he saw it stop this boy in his tracks. He couldn't get through it at all, so he knew he must be a magician of some sort."

"Well, Kitor?" asked the Chief Constable, turning to look at the large, black crow that perched on Clara's shoulder. "What can you tell us about him?"

"I followed him home," Kitor said, ruffling his feathers.

"Wonderful! Where does he live?"

"His name's Lewis and he lives in Heriot Row with his mother and father."

"Lewis Grant! Well, well," the Chief Constable sat back in his chair with a sigh of satisfaction.

"You know him, then?" the Ranger said, looking at Sir Archie in surprise.

"There's a report about the family sitting on my desk at the office," the Chief Constable replied. "This is confidential information that I'm going to give you. Neil, Clara," he looked at them in turn, "you mustn't repeat any of it, you understand?"

They nodded seriously.

"Do you remember all the art thefts that took place a few weeks ago?" he asked. The Macleans nodded, looking puzzled. "Sir James already knows this, but all the valuables stolen, including the *Mona Lisa,* had one thing in common. They all appeared in a book called *Famous Collections of the World.* Only five hundred copies of the book were printed and there were three in Edinburgh. One was owned by a Mr Robinson, so naturally my men checked out the address in Heriot Row." He shook his head. "They didn't have much luck. Mr Robinson is in America and the Grants seemed quite a respectable couple. They've lived in and around the Middle East for years. Lewis was born out there. Robert Grant's an oil-executive and since he's been here, has spent most of his time in Aberdeen. Mrs Grant's mother has been in hospital for months and, well, we found nothing to connect them with the thefts at all."

"So you think that Lewis Grant was responsible for all the thefts?" Sir James interrupted, looking absolutely appalled.

"I'd say so," shrugged the Chief Constable. "The book was in the house, after all, and Kitor says the boy's a magician ..."

"I can't believe it!" Sir James looked upset.

"I told you how the pieces were stolen, James," Sir Archie reminded him, "and it all hangs together. They were stolen by magic and returned by magic. It's the only explanation."

"But why would he return them?" Janet MacLean asked, a puzzled look on her face.

"Maybe he got a fright when the police turned up on the doorstep?" Neil offered.

"I don't see that it really adds up," Sir James objected. "Now, he's going round saving people's lives!"

"That's assuming that he *is* the Shadow," John MacLean added.

"Well," the Chief Constable put down his coffee cup and looked round the little group, "everyone we've interviewed has said, quite definitely, that the Shadow is a boy and there surely can't be two boy magicians in Edinburgh at the same time, can there, Kitor?"

"I shouldn't think so," Kitor croaked, shaking his head.

"Kitor says he goes to George Heriot's," Clara offered.

"Heriot's is just a temporary thing," Sir James interrupted. "The family will all be moving up north come the New Year. Lewis will start school in Aberdeen at the start of next term."

It was Archie Thompson's turn to look surprised. "You know them, James?"

Sir James nodded. "Bob Grant was in my office just a few weeks ago. He's been a friend of mine for years and his company has made a very generous donation to the pantomime."

Neil looked thoughtful. "I don't understand it," he said. "You say they've just come back from the Middle East. So, how come Lewis knows about the MacArthurs? Clara and I wanted to make friends with him so that we could find out a bit more about him but dad wouldn't let us."

"I thought it best to wait until the MacArthurs came back before we did anything about him," the Ranger said hastily. "After all, he might be a friend of theirs trying to get in touch with them and ... well, I didn't think it wise to interfere." He paused. "After all, magic's their business, not ours!"

The Chief Constable looked thoughtful. "You're

right, John," he said. "If Lewis Grant has got himself involved in magic then the MacArthurs *are* the
best people to deal with it." He looked across at Sir
James, "and, as the lad's doing nothing but good
these days, it might be best to keep things on hold
until the MacArthurs get back."

17. Skating on Thin Ice

Time slipped rapidly past, however, and it wasn't until the day before the pantomime that the MacArthurs finally returned to Edinburgh.

By then, Clara and Neil were bubbling with excitement, for the dress rehearsal had gone really well and they just *knew* that *Ali Baba* was going to be the best Christmas show in town. They had, of course, no big part to play but were happy to be in most of the crowd scenes and had also been picked to act as pages to Matt Lafferty, the Grand Vizier to the Sultan, when he appeared on stage. They loved their costumes and the glitz, glamour and fun of taking part in such an exotic production.

Neil, however, still had niggling doubts about Murdo and Wullie and on Saturday afternoon, they'd called their carpets and had gone back to Mary King's Close.

Once again, Clara and Kitor watched anxiously from on high as the ghosts clustered round Neil. They were so frightful, so awful and so friendly!

"I listened to what they crooks were saying for quite a while the other day," the old Codger said chattily to Neil, "and by the sound of it, I think they're planning their robbery for Monday night."

"Monday night?" Neil looked startled, for Monday night was the opening night of the panto-mime.

The old Codger nodded.

"I really don't understand it," Neil said, looking doubtful. "My dad told me that they don't keep money in that bank any more. I even checked it out with my teacher at school and she said exactly the same thing. It's a museum, nowadays. They won't get a penny!"

"You said that before," the old Codger frowned, "but they're still working away. There are three of them now, you know. The new fellow's called Tammy somebody or other ... Tammy Souter, I think the name was."

"Three of them?" Neil was surprised. "We only met Wullie and Murdo!"

Mary King looked at him. "You mean you came into the Underground City and you didn't tell us?" she said, disapprovingly.

"We'd have told you if we'd been able to find you," Neil grinned, apologetically. "We managed to get in through the cellars under the Assembly Hall and, well, to tell you the truth, we got lost. It's like a rabbit warren up there and if it hadn't been for Wullie and Murdo, we might still be wandering round looking for the way out."

"So you met them!" Mr Rafferty looked relieved. "You *did* tell them about the Plague People, didn't you?" he added anxiously.

"Well, actually I didn't," admitted Neil. "I was scared that if I mentioned you and the Plague People, they'd realize that we knew about their plans to rob the bank. We'd been down the alley by then and as they hadn't let loose any of the Plague People I didn't think it necessary ..."

Mr Rafferty flung a weary hand to his forehead. "He didn't think it was necessary!" he repeated. "He didn't think it necessary!"

"Neil! Where are your brains, laddie? Of course it was necessary!" the old Codger said, scratching his head and looking concerned.

"It's just as well we've put in our application," Mr Rafferty said, striding up and down, looking totally distraught. "They've got to be made to leave!"

"Application?" queried Neil.

"When you didn't come back to see us, Neil," Mary King said seriously, "we ... well, we thought we'd scared you off. We didn't know you were still trying to help us and anyway, Mr Rafferty thought it was really up to us to get rid of the crooks on our own."

"Aye, it wasn't fair involving you in our problems," nodded the old Codger.

"We talked it over and in the end we decided to apply to become visible," Mary King said. "It's quite a serious step for us to take, you understand, but the Council of Elders don't want the Plague People to escape either.

"They're a nasty lot, the Plague People," explained the old Codger, "not like us at all. If we tried to stand up to them, they'd attack us and we'd end up losing the little substance we have."

"And once they'd done that, they'd roam the streets of Edinburgh and infect everyone," Mr.Rafferty said, nodding his head worriedly.

"And then there'd be more plague ghosts than ever," added Clarinda, fluttering her hands in distress.

"So it's been agreed that we can materialize. Show ourselves, that is."

"Show yourselves!" Neil gulped, his eyes wide with apprehension as a vision of coach-loads of panic-stricken tourists screaming down the High Street, flitted through his mind. "You ... you can't do that! You'll give everyone heart attacks! You ... you just don't now how scary you look!"

Mary King looked up sharply. "That's the whole idea," she replied. "We want to frighten Murdo and his friends so that they'll give up the idea of robbing the bank, leave the Underground City and never, ever come back."

She was quite firm about it and Neil could see that nothing was going to shift her. He ran his hand through his dark hair and shook his head. "Well," he said, still horrified at the thought, "I ... I hope it all comes off."

"Thank you, anyway, for trying to help, Neil," the old Codger said. "If you ever visit us again we promise we won't try to scare *you!*"

All the ghosts laughed at this joke and Neil smiled weakly. "Thanks," he said, as he got on his carpet, "and good luck!"

They talked about it round the fire when they got home. Kitor looked worried and Clara was still a bit white. She'd hated it when all the ghosts had laughed. "You know, I really feel quite sorry for the crooks," she said. "I quite liked Wullie!"

"I only hope he has a strong heart," said Neil. "Just imagine having all those ghosts flapping round the place. They'll scare him to death!"

As if their worries about the ghosts weren't enough, the next day they met Lewis Grant! Purely, as they thought, by accident.

Snow had fallen overnight and Edinburgh was layered in deep drifts. The city was like a winter wonderland. Crusted in white, the castle reared on high like a picture out of a fairy-tale; the gardens below were strung with lights as children and adults alike, skated on the outdoor ice-rink and a multitude of vendors did a roaring trade in hot dogs, hamburgers, roasted chestnuts and steaming mugs of hot chocolate and mulled wine.

The Grants were there with Lewis. After a life spent in the desert, the snow was very much a novelty and as they tottered unsteadily round the rink, Lewis looked enviously at a pretty girl and a dark-haired boy who glided effortlessly through the crowds.

"These children have magic in them, Lewis," Casimir said suddenly.

"Have they?" Lewis perked up at once, looking at them with interest. "I think I'd like to get to know them," he decided.

"So would I," Casimir said softly, promptly taking charge of proceedings. It was no accident, therefore, that Lewis managed to lose his precarious balance and, legs and arms waving wildly, thumped down on the ice just as Neil and Clara skated up. And it was a hex that made Clara stop and help him to his feet.

Neil took his other arm and, supporting him on either side, they skated with him round the rink until he got into the rhythm. Lewis grinned his

thanks as Neil gave him tips and to his amazement, he soon found that he could skate quite
well. Full of new-found confidence, he waved to his
mother and father as they passed.

Bob Grant beckoned them over. "Your mother
fancies some mulled wine, Lewis," he said, as they
came to an impressive stop beside him, showering
ice everywhere. "How would you like some hot
chocolate?" His glance included all three of them
but that wasn't what left Neil and Clara totally
gob-smacked. Lewis! They hadn't thought to ask
his name. Could this be the boy Kitor had seen on
the hill? Could this be Lewis Grant? He certainly
fitted Kitor's description.

Although Neil and Clara managed to cover their
astonishment pretty well, Lewis noticed their
hesitation. "It's okay," he said, "this is my dad and
that's my mum over there."

"I'm Bob Grant," his father said, shaking their
hands as Neil and Clara introduced themselves.

Clara smiled shyly. "Thanks, Mr Grant," she
said politely, trying to hide the fact that her
thoughts were in turmoil. Lewis Grant! It must
be him, she decided. "We'd love some, wouldn't we
Neil?" she added, turning to look meaningfully at
her brother.

Neil nodded but as they made their way towards
the stall he was busy trying to work out just how
much magic had been involved in their "accidental"
meeting and, looking at Clara, knew from her face
that she was wondering much the same thing!

"They didn't have all this when I was your age,"
Bob Grant said, gesturing towards the ice-rink as

he dished out mugs of steaming chocolate. "No ice-rink and no Christmas Market either," he said looking further along the gardens to where the stalls of the German Market blazed in a myriad of bright decorations.

Christmas carols drifted on the frosty air as they turned to look at the picturesque scene. The huge Christmas tree at the top of the Mound glittered in a spangle of lights, and even the towering spires of the Assembly Hall were softened by their icing of snow.

"That's where the pantomime's being held, Lewis," his mother said. "In that big building up there." She turned to Clara. "I hope you're both going to see *Ali Baba,*" she said kindly. "I think it's going to be a lot of fun!"

"Actually, we're in it," Neil admitted. "We don't have any real parts, though," he said hurriedly, "we're in the crowd scenes and things like that."

Lewis looked envious. "That sounds great," he said. "We're going to see it tomorrow night, so we'll look out for you!"

"Tomorrow's the first night!" Neil said. "We're hoping it all goes well!"

"It's fabulous," Clara said. "You'll have a great time!"

"I forgot to mention it, Lewis," his father said, "but we'll be going backstage after the show so if you like, you can meet up with Neil and Clara then. Sir James is an old friend of mine," he explained, "and he's invited us to meet Matt Lafferty. He seems to be the star."

Lewis's face lit up. "That'd be fab!" he grinned. "You know, I'm really glad we've met."

"Great!" grinned Neil, gulping down the last of his drink. "Now, how about practising your skating some more? He's getting quite good, isn't he, Clara?"

Lewis nodded eagerly at this suggestion and with a final wave of thanks to Mr and Mrs Grant, they moved back on to the ice and were soon lost in the crowd.

Unseen by them all, Kitor sat in the black, bare branches of a nearby tree, utterly frozen and not, it must be added, with the cold. Kitor was absolutely stiff with fear! He had flown across from Arthur's Seat not only to watch Neil and Clara skating but also to enjoy the lights, the Christmas decorations and the excited crowds that thronged Princes Street Gardens ... not to mention, of course, the added treat of any left-over scraps of hot dogs and hamburgers!

Soaring in over the gardens, Kitor had very nearly had heart-failure when he'd spotted Neil and Clara skating round the rink with Lewis Grant in tow. How they'd met, he didn't know, but was quite sure it wasn't by chance. He watched them with a sinking heart, for he knew that it was up to him to find out all about this boy who had been trying to get into the hill. It would be the first thing the MacArthur would want to know.

Magicians, however, are in a class of their own and are definitely not to be trifled with. Kitor, therefore, steeled himself grimly and it was with a fast-beating heart that he managed to sidle unnoticed up to the Grants while they sipped their warm drinks.

Now, although Casimir had been careful to hide himself from Neil and Clara, he couldn't hide his presence from the world of magic. Kitor immediately sensed the strength of power emanating from Lewis and almost choked as recognition dawned.

He knew immediately who the magician inside Lewis was. Prince Casimir! Prince Casimir had returned!

The magician, however, seemed to sense that something was amiss and even as Kitor saw the boy's head turn to look searchingly among the crowd, the crow scuttled hastily behind a pile of carrier bags, loaded with presents, and it was only when the three children took to the ice again and started skating round that he breathed a heartfelt sigh of relief. Casimir hadn't seen him although he had suspected his presence. Shaking with fright, he fluttered into the trees and, cowering behind the thickest branch he could find, pondered his next move.

18. The MacArthurs' Return

It was only when darkness fell and Princes Street Gardens closed for the night that Kitor swooped carefully from his perch and, keeping to the shadows, flew towards the dark bulk of Arthur's Seat. He was well aware of the peril he was in and heaved a huge sigh of relief as he reached the hill for, had Casimir been aware of him, he was quite sure that a thunderbolt would have long since finished him off.

He flew to the shaft that the pigeons used to enter the hill and dropped thankfully down into the darkness below. At last, he was safe! Completely safe! No thunderbolt could reach him now, for the magic shield that the MacArthurs had put round the hill protected all within it.

As he flapped his wings at the bottom of the shaft, he suddenly realized that the hill was filled with light. Torches were burning everywhere and the cavern was full of people. The MacArthurs! Kitor could hardly believe his luck! They had returned!

Heads turned to look at him curiously as he flew towards the huge chair layered with banks of cushions that held the MacArthur himself. A small, but regal figure, the MacArthur sat, straight and imperious, in a red, fur-lined coat and long, black boots. This vaguely Russian outfit was topped by a fur hat that sported long, drooping flaps that covered his ears and a tartan scarf. Braziers were being lit throughout the cavern but the hill, empty for so long, was still bitterly cold and, despite his feathers, Kitor shivered.

The MacArthur watched as Kitor flew towards him and knew, just by looking at him, that the bird bore urgent news.

"Welcome back, MacArthur," Kitor croaked, bowing low before collapsing weakly in a shaking heap of feathers.

Hamish and Jaikie put down the brazier they were carrying and strode up to where Kitor trembled pathetically in front of the MacArthur.

"What is it, Kitor?" Hamish asked, lifting an eyebrow at the MacArthur, who looked puzzled and shook his head. "What's happened?"

"Prince Casimir!" the bird stuttered. "Prince Casimir has returned!"

There was a horrified silence. "Prince Casimir?" the MacArthur said, sitting up straight in complete disbelief, "but surely Prince Casimir is dead?"

Jaikie looked at Kitor, who, adjusting his ruffled feathers, was struggling to his feet. "Are you sure?" he asked, lifting the bird gently onto a cushion and gesturing to one of the men to light the brazier and bring it closer.

"It was Prince Casimir," the crow said stubbornly. "I knew him at once."

They looked at one another in consternation, believing him implicitly, for Kitor had once belonged to Casimir's son, Prince Kalman. There was no way Kitor was going to mistake Casimir's presence.

The MacArthur looked appalled. "Jaikie, you'd better go to Arthur's cave and fetch Archie. He'll need to be in on this!"

Archie and Arthur arrived together and when Archie had perched himself comfortably on the great dragon's arm, Kitor poured out his story of how he had seen the boy on the hill trying to break through the protective shield and told them, too, of his exploits as the Shadow.

The MacArthurs looked at one another in amazement. "You must be joking, Kitor," Archie said, looking absolutely thunderstruck. "Are you seriously trying to tell us that Casimir, Casimir of all people, is involved in saving people's lives all over the country?"

Kitor sighed. "That's one reason I got such a shock when I found out that it was Casimir inside Lewis," the bird admitted doubtfully. He drew a deep breath. "It's ... well, it's not the sort of thing he ever did, is it?"

"You can say that again," muttered Hamish. "The Casimir *I* know would never have lifted a finger to help anyone."

"It's certainly a turn up for the books!" Jaikie said, disbelief written all over him. "Let's face it, Casimir was always as proud as Lucifer. That's why I could never understand why he stole the Sultan's crown. When you think about it, it was totally out of character ..."

"Yes," agreed the MacArthur, with a puzzled frown, "I've always thought there was something a bit strange about the whole affair."

"The Chief Constable said that the Grants had

just come back from the Middle East," offered Kitor.

Archie's head jerked. "That could be where Casimir managed to take Lewis over!" he said excitedly.

The MacArthur nodded in sudden understanding. "It's possible," he agreed.

"But we all assumed that when Casimir stole the Sultan's Crown, the storm carriers chased him and killed him!" objected Jaikie.

"Hasn't the Sultan mentioned Prince Casimir to you at all?" questioned Hamish dubiously.

The MacArthur shook his head. "The Sultan has never mentioned him," he confessed, "and, quite frankly, I didn't like to bring the subject up."

"Then it's possible that the storm carriers *didn't* kill him when he stole the crown. The Sultan must have imprisoned him instead. Probably out in the desert somewhere ..."

"If anything," Archie mused, "you'd think Casimir would be spending his time looking for Kalman instead of indulging in this Shadow business! Kalman is his son, after all!"

Jaikie sat up. "Maybe that would explain why he was trying to get into the hill," he said, excitedly. "If he's discovered that Ardray is no more, he'd want to find out what happened to Kalman and I bet he'd rather come to us for information than go to Morven and the Lords of the North. You used to get on with him better than most, MacArthur, if I remember rightly!"

"The other thing you should know, MacArthur," Kitor said, "is that Neil and Clara have been among the ghosts in the old town."

The MacArthur frowned. "You should have told them to have nothing to do with them, Kitor," he said, sternly. "Ghosts are something else! How did their parents allow it?"

"They didn't tell them," Kitor admitted. "The MacLeans know nothing about it. But it wasn't Neil's fault. The ghosts asked him to help them."

Jaikie blinked. "This gets weirder and weirder!" he said, in amazement. "The ghosts asked Neil to help them? I've never heard the like of it!"

"The Plague People," Kitor said. "They were afraid of them getting out."

There was a deadly silence. "The Plague People?" the MacArthur said in surprise. "I thought they'd been sealed up pretty firmly." Nevertheless, a shade of concern crossed his face as he spoke and he looked thoughtful.

"The ghosts are worried. There are some men working in the Underground City. They're trying to break into the vaults of the big bank on the Mound. Neil says that the bank doesn't keep money there any more so they won't get anything, but the thing is that they're very near the Plague People," Kitor paused, "and we all know what *they're* like!"

The MacArthur shuddered. "Aye, well, that's not our business," he said. "The ghosts will have to take care of the Plague People themselves."

"I think they are," Kitor nodded. "The last time we were there, they told Neil they were going to try to scare the wits out of the crooks. They've … they've asked for permission to materialize!"

Jaikie and Archie looked at one another. "That's

a bit much, isn't it?" muttered Jaikie, raising his eyebrows. "They'll scare Edinburgh stupid!"

Kitor nodded. "They're pretty awful," he said doubtfully, "but I don't think they plan to leave the Underground City. And the Chief Constable said that he was going to wait until you got back so that you could work out what to do about Lewis."

The MacArthur nodded approvingly. "I think we'd better all meet up," he said, "and the sooner the better! Hamish, take a carpet and tell the Ranger what has happened so that he can pass the word on to Sir James and the Chief Constable. In the meantime, I'll speak to the Sultan and Lord Rothlan through the crystal. They'll both have to know that Casimir has escaped."

A strong undercurrent of excitement ran through the little group as, later that evening, they sat round the MacArthur's chair. How often, Clara thought as she sat with Kitor on her shoulder, had they sat like this in the past, sprawled on cushions and low divans listening to the MacArthur. Arthur, the great dragon, lay beside them, occasionally blowing gusts of roaring, sparkling flame across the cavern, for the huge hall was still fairly cold, despite the glowing braziers that had been dotted here and there.

"I've told the Sultan everything," explained the MacArthur, looking round the assembled company. "Needless to say, he's not best pleased that Casimir has managed to escape."

"Is he coming here," queried Hamish, "to the hill?"

A sudden silence fell as the MacArthur nodded. "He plans to come tomorrow evening to sort things out."

"I'll do anything I can to help!" Sir James said frankly. "And if we can somehow get Casimir to leave Lewis before the Sultan arrives, then so much the better. As it happens, I've already invited the Grants backstage after the show."

"Lewis told us," nodded Neil. "We met him at the ice rink in Princes Street Gardens and he's looking forward to seeing us again, isn't he Clara? I'm sure we could find some excuse to get him to leave his mum and dad. We could show him our dressing-room, or something. Then you could talk to him on your own, Sir James, and tell him that the MacArthur wants to talk to him. What do you think, Dad?" he asked, turning to his father.

"A good idea," the Ranger nodded.

"It might be managed," the Chief Constable said thoughtfully.

"He's a wily old bird, is Casimir," the MacArthur interrupted. "I reckon he'll play things by ear. After all, he tried to get into the hill to speak to me, didn't he? He'll take you up on it all right, James — to see what I have to offer, if nothing else."

Jaikie looked doubtful. "Do we have anything to offer?" he queried.

The MacArthur looked grim. "I think," he said, "that the Sultan might be willing to pardon Prince Casimir now that he has his crown back."

"Great!" Archie looked relieved and Arthur blew an approving cloud of smoke from his nostrils that set everybody coughing.

After that, the party broke up and as the magic carpets soared into the air, Kitor flew to the MacArthur's shoulder to remind him of the ghosts of Mary King's Close.

The MacArthur nodded and quietly drew the Chief Constable to one side. "The Bank of Scotland on the Mound, Sir Archie," he said. "I've heard a whisper that some bank robbers are interested in cleaning it out."

Archie Thompson's eyebrows rose in surprise. "They must be pretty thick, then," he replied. "It's not been a working branch for quite a while now."

"Then you're not worried about it?"

The Chief Constable shook his head. "It's a museum these days," he replied.

"That's what Neil said," nodded the MacArthur.

The Chief Constable's eyes sharpened at the mention of Neil's name. "Actually, the Bank of Scotland has donated quite a lot of money to *Ali Baba*. They always contribute to good causes and it so happens that Molly and I are going to see the pantomime tomorrow night with one of the bank's directors. I'll … er, sound MacPherson out, then."

19. Overture and Beginners

The Assembly Hall that evening was a scene of hustle and bustle as the cast of *Ali Baba and the Forty Thieves* arrived early and settled nervously in their dressing rooms to apply the layers of make-up and greasepaint that would transform them from solid Scots into the more exotic characters of the pantomime. For the stars who had dressing rooms of their own, this was more or less a routine matter but for the bit-part players it was all new, thrilling and exciting.

Neil and Clara found themselves squashed in the corner of a large room that was totally overcrowded. The brightly-lit stretch of mirrors above the make-up shelf that ran the length of the room added to the confusion, not only reflecting the performers but also rack upon rack of gaudy costumes, magnificent turbans, fancy wigs and those ornate slippers with turned-up toes so popular among the peoples of the east.

"I'll be lucky if I can keep these slippers on my feet," muttered Neil, as a make-up artist plastered Clara's fair skin with what looked like brown gunge. "I'll have to hold them on with my toes, I think!"

"I saw mum in the wardrobe room. She might be able to give you something to tie round them," Clara mumbled, trying to keep her lips still as the woman doing her face wielded sticks of make-up and hissed at her not to talk.

Neil made his way to the door through the chattering, excited crowd that milled here and there between the costumes and the mirrors. He couldn't see his mother anywhere in the general pandemonium of the dressing rooms. It all looked pretty frantic, but rehearsals had taught him that there was method behind the madness and that within an hour the entire cast would be totally transformed. Reaching the side of the stage, he practised walking up and down to get the feel of the gaudy slippers. Before he had arrived at the theatre he had been looking forward to taking part in the show; now his confidence drained away as he worried about keeping the shoes on his feet!

Last minute practices were still going on. On stage, two men were fighting with deadly-looking, curved scimitars. Neil grinned as he watched them go through their routine. Before the rehearsals started, neither man had ever used a sword before, far less a scimitar, but they had managed to work out a mock-duel with the help of the one man in the cast that knew anything about sword-play; Alec Johnston, the Genie of the Lamp.

Alec, whose arrogance was unsurpassed, considered himself a rising star in the theatrical world and had, unsurprisingly, managed to make more enemies than friends during the course of rehearsals. Nevertheless, he was a professional and stood watching the fight critically as the two swordsmen went through their paces.

He was already made-up and in costume. It was, Neil admitted enviously, a fantastic costume. A dark blue mask, spiked with gold, decorated the

upper part of his face and covered his hair while
a loose cloak of the same colour hung over a tight
under-suit of shimmering gold. And there was no
doubt whatsoever that his spectacular leap onto
the stage when Ali Baba rubbed the magic lamp,
was absolutely fantastic and one of the highlights
of the pantomime. However much you disliked
him as a person, he made a fantastic genie, Neil
thought, as he saw him lift a commanding hand
and stop the fight.

"Watch me again," he instructed, taking the
scimitar from the hands of one of the men. "Step
forward — one, two, three — and then lunge, like
this." The steel blade glinted and as the folds of his
shimmering cloak rippled and billowed, his arm
swung forward with deadly accuracy.

In the wings, the producer looked at his watch
and turned to the Stage Manager. "Has the paint
on that big mirror dried yet?" he asked.

"Should've done! I'll just get Sandy and Alfie to
bring it upstairs. It weighs a ton and a half!"

Neil barely heard them as he turned to go back
to the dressing room. He hadn't been made up yet
and reckoned that Clara must be nearly finished.
In his anxiety to get back, however, Neil missed
a sight that would have set his pulses racing; for
barely five minutes later, two burly stage hands
carried a huge mirror up the stairs from the cellar.
Casimir, the Sultan, the MacArthurs, Sir James
— all of them would have recognized it immediately. It was over seven feet tall and its iron frame
was decorated with carvings of flowers, birds and
strange animals. It was a magic mirror!

The paint shop had done a grand job the Stage Manager thought as he looked it over; the drab frame, now covered in layers of gold paint, shone brilliantly and its mirrored surface, he reckoned, would reflect the stage lighting nicely. It had been a real find and just what was needed to give an extra buzz to the bazaar scene. Had he known just how big a buzz the mirror was going to give the bazaar scene, he would have sent it straight back down to the cellars there and then but, as he didn't, he waved a casual hand. "Stack it in that corner over there," he told Alfie. "We're using it for the Lashkari Bazaar scene!"

"Sorry I'm late," Jock MacPherson apologized as he squeezed along the row of people to sit beside his wife. "I got held up at the bank!"

Archie Thompson gave a wry smile as Jock settled in his seat with a sigh, glad he'd made it before the performance began. How often, thought the Chief Constable, had he been in the same position himself! He looked at his watch. "Still five minutes to curtain-up, Jock," he said comfortably. "Busy, these days, are you?"

"Frantically," was the reply, "been doing nothing but sign papers all evening. We're modernizing a lot of the branches at the moment and while it saves time to do them all in one fell swoop, so to speak, the amount of organization is tremendous. Got to stash the cash somewhere, eh!"

Sir Archie's eyes sharpened and a stab of worry shot through him. "May I ask where you've ... er ... stashed it?"

Jock MacPherson turned in his seat and looked him warily in the eye. "Do you have a reason for asking, Archie?"

The Chief Constable nodded. "I do, as it happens."

"In the vaults on the Mound."

Archie Thompson paled and reached for his mobile. "How much?" he asked.

"Well … millions," was the somewhat guarded reply.

"The devil there is," muttered the Chief Constable as he got to his feet. "Come on, Jock. I'll catch up with you at the bank! If my information is correct, we're in for a busy night!"

The Chief Constable wasted no time. He flashed his ID at the pass door, headed back stage and collared the first person in authority that he saw.

"Where are the two kids that act as pages to Matt Lafferty?" he asked the Stage Manager.

Neil, however, had seen the Chief Constable. "Sir Archie's here," he whispered to Clara as the Stage Manager pointed in their direction.

"I think he wants to talk to us," Clara said as the kilted figure strode towards them.

"Neil," Sir Archie said, drawing them to one side and coming straight to the point, "what do you know about the bank robbers that are planning to rob the bank on the Mound?"

Neil looked startled. This was quite a different Sir Archie to the one they knew. He was using his official voice and it was obvious that the matter was urgent.

"They've found a way into the bank through the Underground City," he replied. "They've got an old map that shows all the streets."

"They get in through the cellars of Deacon Brodie's Tavern," Clara added, "and they've cleared all the alleyways down to the bank."

"You don't, by any chance, know who they are and when they plan to carry out this robbery, do you?" queried Sir Archie.

"Well, I think it *might* have been planned for tonight," Neil said hesitantly, remembering what the old Codger had said. "But they won't get anything, will they?" he added doubtfully. "Dad told me that the building's a museum."

"Can you describe the men to me?"

"There are two of them," Neil answered. "Murdo and Wullie."

"That pair!" muttered the Chief Constable.

"And there's a third man now called Tammy Souter," added Clara. "At least that's what the ghosts said."

"Tammy Souter?" exclaimed Sir Archie, "well, well," he said, punching numbers into his mobile, "we know all about *him!*" Then he stopped and did a spectacular double-take. "That's what *who* said?" he asked, in disbelief.

"The ghosts from Mary King's Close," Neil answered. "They're not really worried about the bank but they're afraid the crooks might let the Plague People out by mistake. The cellars that hold them are quite close to where they're working."

"It's the Plague People they're worried about," Clara nodded, looking scared. "Mary King said that if they get out they'll … they'll bring the Black Death back to Edinburgh!"

20. The Big Bang

I won't tell you what Murdo, Wullie and Tammy Souter said when they first clapped eyes on the ghosts but to say that they used very, very bad language is putting it mildly! Mind you, they were scared out of their minds, which I suppose is some excuse. Murdo, certainly, turned as white as a sheet and Tammy Souter looked much the same, if not worse.

Wullie was actually too scared to speak at all. He just looked utterly petrified as the ghosts, now visible, floated through the walls and drifted down the alleys in all their dreadful glory. Pressing himself against the wall of one of the houses, he covered his face with his hands and peered out between his fingers as the ghosts howled around them in freezing blasts of cold air. Murdo took a swing at them with his pick and Tammy tried walloping them with a shovel but it didn't do any good, for although the ghosts looked solid enough, they were misty and insubstantial at the same time.

Wullie gave a horrified moan as an old hag screamed threateningly in front of him, her empty eyes staring and her clawed hands grasping at his face. It was too much. He let out a yell of terror and took off into the alleys at a speed that would have put an Olympic runner to shame. Murdo saw him go and with a muttered curse, dropped his pick and charged after him.

"Wullie, you fool," he yelled, "Wullie, come back here, will you!"

Wullie, totally panic-stricken, took not the slightest bit of notice and streaked unseeing through the narrow streets of the Underground City. Such was his blind terror that he neither knew nor cared where he was going nor, as it happened, where he was putting his feet, and, as the rubble-strewn alleys were an open invitation to disaster, it wasn't long before his headlong flight was brought to an abrupt end when he tripped over a scatter of bricks and fell flat on his face.

Murdo ran up, panting and cursing furiously. He grabbed him by the scruff of the neck and heaved him up. "You gormless idiot," he panted. "You complete nutter! Where do you think you're going? Get lost in these alleys and you'll never find your way out!"

Wullie started to shake. "It's the ghosts," he snuffled tearfully. "I'm scared, Murdo!"

"We're all scared," Murdo confessed, "but, don't you understand, we've got to stick together. If they separate us and get us on our own, it'll be a lot more than scary, believe me!"

Wullie, six feet of shivering terror, stood undecided but it was the thought of being lost, alone and at the mercy of the ghosts that eventually served to concentrate his mind and, although petrified, he saw the point of what Murdo was saying. "Aye," he quavered, "you're maybe right at that!"

"I *am* right," asserted Murdo grimly. "Now come on!" he urged. "We've got to stand by Tammy Souter or he'll never help us do a job again!"

They found Tammy Souter curled up on the floor of the alley surrounded by a hoard of screaming ghosts. The noise they were making was something awful. Wullie stopped and seemed to change his mind about walking any further.

"Look," Murdo said urgently, giving him a shake, "just look at them! They can howl and scream all they like but, think about it, Wullie; nothing's really changed."

"Whatdoyoumean?" moaned a petrified Wullie.

"The only difference is that we can see them and hear them," Murdo said patiently. "I know they're enough to scare the life out of anybody but they're not able to do anything to us, are they? Look at Tammy! All they're doing is screaming their heads off at him!"

And Wullie had to admit, albeit reluctantly, that this was, indeed, the case.

Murdo strode through the ghosts and yanked a petrified Tammy Souter to his feet. "That's enough, Tammy," he said in a voice of steel. "These ghosts can make all the racket they like but haven't you realized yet that they can't hurt us? Now, you've got a job to do. Get on with it!" And with that, he pushed a fearful Tammy towards the massive hole in the red-brick wall where the metal casing of the vault gleamed dully in the dim light of the lantern.

"You get on with your job," Murdo said abruptly, "and Wullie and I will stand at your back. We'll no' let the ghosts near you. Okay?"

"Aye," said Wullie, trying to sound brave. "We'll protect you, Tammy!"

"And the quicker you are, the quicker we'll be out of here!" snapped Murdo.

Now, Tammy Souter had always prided himself on his quick, neat work. He was a pro and valued his reputation. Not only that, he could already hear himself boasting in the pub for years to come about the night he did a bank job with ghosts howling at his elbow. The thought of the pub did much to calm his trembling nerves and helped him bring his mind to bear on the vault. Shutting out the fiendish howls of the ghosts, his nimble fingers went to work until the explosives were in place. "Nearly finished," he muttered, "just the fuse and the detonator to go!"

Mary King, when she appeared, did not notice the detonator and, indeed, wouldn't have known what it was, even if she had.

Murdo knew that something was going on when the ghosts stopped their banshee wailing and fell quiet. He looked up the alley and saw a little group of ghosts approaching. The leader was a woman wearing a long dress, a shawl and a bonnet. She stopped about three feet from them and all the ghosts crowded in behind her.

"My name's Mary King," she said.

"Really?" Murdo looked at her in surprise. He had heard of Mary King's Close. Indeed, it was marked on his map.

"I must ask you to leave the Underground City," she said sternly. "You don't know it but you are very close to the cellars where the ghosts of the Plague People are imprisoned."

"The Plague People?" Murdo stiffened and

looked at her in dawning understanding. He had wondered at the meaning of the tiny skull and crossbone drawings that decorated part of his map.

"They mustn't get out," she said. "They sense that you are close to them, you know, and are desperate to be free! If they *do* get out, they will infect you and the city with the Black Death. Do you understand?"

Murdo nodded uneasily. The plague! His blood ran cold at the very mention of the word. "Look, lady," he began. "Er, I mean, look, Mrs King, we've nearly finished here and we'll be gone in about half an hour. We won't disturb your Plague People, I assure you and we won't come back!"

"I have your word on that?"

Murdo nodded. "You have my word," he said.

Murdo's word was not, however, what you might call the word of a gentleman. He and Wullie had spent many long hours clearing the alley of rubble and no way was he going to leave the Underground City without the money that lay in the vault.

Mary King, who had inspected the alleyway on her way down, now looked at the hole in the red-brick wall with a sigh of relief. There really didn't seem to be much damage at all. She nodded. "In that case we will leave you," she said and, with a wave of her hands, she dispersed the ghosts — leaving Murdo, Wullie and Tammy to watch in awe as they drifted off along the dimly lit passages and through the walls of the houses until not one remained.

"Right," said Tammy when they were on their own once more. "You'd better take cover while I blow the charge!"

"Er, how much damage will it do?" queried Murdo, mindful of the mention of the Plague People. He gestured to the ceiling above his head. "It won't bring this lot down on us, will it?"

Tammy looked at him. "Do me a favour, Murdo!" he said. "What do you take me for?"

The explosion was more of a dull thump than a big bang but the shock waves that swept through the Underground City, blew the startled ghosts in all directions. The houses in the narrow alleys quivered and shook under the force of the blast and here and there, cracks appeared and walls crumbled.

The ghosts gathered in fury as they realized what must have happened but Murdo, Wullie and Tammy Souter had forgotten all about them as they waited for the dust to settle before they rushed towards the bank.

21. The Lashkari Bazaar

The first act of the pantomime had been a stunning success and as the curtain rose for the second act, there were gasps from the audience and a spontaneous round of applause, for the set of the Lashkari Bazaar was a glittering confection of oriental splendour. Against a background of blue sky, palm trees and the odd minaret, gold glittered everywhere. Colourfully-dressed vendors hawked their wares from stalls heaped high with goods and pedlars in satin waistcoats and baggy trousers, wandered among them, selling ribbons, trinkets and scarves. The bazaar was also a slave-market and as the curtain rose, the throne on a raised dais to the right of the stage, was being draped in cloth of gold in preparation for the imminent arrival of the Sultan himself.

Matt Lafferty, gorgeously attired in turban, black boots, breeches and the dark purple robes of the Grand Vizier, was in charge of this operation and strode the stage commandingly, staff in hand, his cloak swirling dramatically behind him. His pages, Neil and Clara, armed with wicked-looking, tall spears, wore turbans, tunics and trousers striped in purple and gold.

Matt Lafferty, by this time, had the audience in the palm of his hand; they loved him, roared with laughter at all his jokes and, despite the fact that *Ali Baba* was supposedly set in

Turkey, found nothing unusual in his broad Scots accent.

"Where are they then, ye great oaf?" he shouted, waving his fearsome staff of office at the huge figure of the slave-merchant. "His Magnificence will be here ony minute! Move it, will ye! Get thae lassies ower here, pronto," he thundered.

It was while the slave-girls were being dragged on that Clara, her eyes roving idly round the stalls in the bazaar, spotted the magic mirror. Her eyes widened in amazement and her heart started to pound. Despite the paint job, she knew it immediately for what it was. A magic mirror! Neil was standing on the other side of the dais and she longed to attract his attention. But she daren't! She had to stand quietly, looking straight ahead of her during this bit of the scene. Where on earth had the mirror come from, she wondered. She could have sworn it hadn't been there during the dress rehearsal. And as Ali Baba nipped among the stalls in the market-place, looking for a way to free his girlfriend, Morgana, from the wicked slave-merchant, she wished the scene were over. The MacArthur had to be told about this as soon as possible. *And* the Sultan, she thought, for wasn't he due to arrive this very evening from Turkey? Her thoughts were in turmoil.

It wasn't only Clara who had spotted the magic mirror, however. Casimir homed in on it right away and got such a shock that Lewis sat bolt upright in his seat.

"Are you all right, Lewis?" his mother asked in concern.

"I … I think I have to go to the loo," he whispered to her. It was Casimir speaking, not him, but since his mother thought he had spoken, he more or less had to go.

"You should have gone at the interval," she said a trifle crossly at the thought of him having to push his way along the row, disturbing people who were comfortably settled.

"I have to go, Mum. It … it must have been something I ate!"

"Don't be long, then. You're missing the show!"

Lewis nodded and apologizing profusely made his way along the row and out into the corridor.

Once in the Gents he headed straight for the mirrors. "Show yourself, Casimir!" he demanded.

Casimir immediately appeared, his normally rather grumpy, old face shining with a mixture of hope and excitement.

"Look, Casimir," Lewis told him frankly, "if it's another Shadow thing, I don't want to know about it! Let the police deal with it for a change. I want to watch *Ali Baba* and right now I'm missing one of the best bits!"

"Didn't you see it, Master? Didn't you see it on the stage?"

"Didn't I see what on the stage?"

"The mirror, Master! The magic mirror. How could you miss it?"

Lewis frowned and heaved a sigh. He could see from his face that Casimir was in raptures. He was almost crying, blast him! What a time to see the magic mirror! "For heaven's sake," he said, "couldn't you have waited until the end of the act to tell me? We can't do anything just now, Casimir, not in the middle of the show, we can't! You've dragged me out here for nothing!"

Sir James, as it happened, had spotted the magic mirror as well and as the shock wore off, wondered frantically what he was going to do. Like Clara, he knew that the MacArthur and the Sultan should be told as soon as possible but he found himself in an awkward predicament. He just couldn't get up and walk out in the middle of the act — it was his production, after all, and would cause comment. People would gossip!

Trying not to be obvious about it, Sir James looked round to where Archie Thompson was seated and to his amazement saw that his seat was empty. Where on earth, he thought, had Archie got to? He knew that the Ranger was on the other side of the aisle but there was little chance of attracting his attention from this distance! He shot a hopeless glance in his direction and saw to his relief that the Ranger was leaning forward and looking at him. Relief swept through Sir James as the Ranger jabbed a finger at the stage. Sir James mouthed the word "MacArthur" at him and received an understanding nod in return. Seconds later he saw the Ranger creep unobtrusively out of the theatre and, mind racing, relaxed in his seat.

While the Ranger, resplendent in kilt and velvet jacket (for all the men were in evening dress) hastened outside to call his carpet, Casimir and Lewis were still in the Gents arguing about the magic mirror.

"Just take me backstage, Master," pleaded

Casimir, "that's all I ask! I promised that if you helped me get my son back that I'd leave you for good. Take me backstage and I'll hide in some pot or jar and then, when the pantomime's over, I can try and get Kalman out of the mirror. Please, Master!"

"I can't take you backstage during the performance, you idiot!" snapped Lewis. "There's a pass door but it'll most likely be locked and if it isn't then there's bound to be somebody on duty to check who wants through!"

"No problem! I'll make us invisible," Casimir promised. "Just think, Master, you'll be rid of me for good!"

"Yes," muttered Lewis, "but you know, Casimir, I've sort of got used to having you hanging around."

"Princes," snapped Casimir irately, "do not 'hang around' as you put it!"

"You know what I mean," Lewis grinned, totally unfazed. "We've been through a lot together and, well … I'll be sorry to see you go."

A feeling of affection swept through Casimir for despite being bored to tears at Lewis's total lack of interest in anything other than comics and pop music, he found that he was going to miss him, too. "I'll miss you, too, Lewis," he said in surprise. "I can't really think why, though!"

"Thanks for nothing," muttered Lewis. He felt a trifle peeved but gave a wry smile, the comment was so utterly typical.

"My last request!" Casimir urged, seeing his smile. "Please, Master!"

Lewis heaved a sigh. "Oh, come on, then," he said in exasperation. "Make me invisible and we'll go backstage but don't forget to reverse the spell so that I can go back to my seat, will you. Otherwise my mother will totally freak!"

Lewis promptly disappeared and, seconds later, the door of the Gents swung open and shut as he made his way to the pass door that separates backstage from Front of House. It was locked, as Lewis had said, but it opened to his gentle tap and he was able to slip through quietly as the door-keeper peered curiously around, wondering if his ears had been playing tricks on him. Backstage was a completely different world and he was immediately absorbed in its alien noises, sounds and smells.

Lewis made his invisible way towards the prompt corner where the Stage Manager, blissfully unaware of the mind-boggling surprises that lay in store for him, joined in the laughter as Matt Lafferty continued to reduce the audience to tears of helpless mirth. Lewis then wandered across the stage, looked at some of the stalls and went up close to the mirror itself, running his hands over the strange carvings.

"Don't touch the carvings, Lewis!" Casimir warned urgently. His warning came too late, however. Lewis had never seen a magic mirror before and was totally amazed when a carved rose slipped under his fingers. As the rose clicked round, the mirror gave a slight hum as though its power supply had suddenly been switched on.

"Whoops!" he whispered, knowing that the mirror, in some strange way, had come to life.

"Well done, Lewis!" Casimir said sourly. "Now before you cause any more damage, perhaps you could find something for me to hide in!"

Lewis, who had spotted an Aladdin's Lamp on one of the stalls, moved towards it. "Just the thing for you, Casimir," he said softly as he put an invisible hand over its spout.

The choice of the lamp, it must be said, wasn't really Lewis's fault. He'd never seen *Ali Baba* before and wasn't to know that in this particular production, the lamp played an important part. Nor did he realize that by putting a genie in it he had quite successfully sabotaged the whole performance — for between them, the magic mirror and the magic lamp were the equivalent of a ticking time bomb. A time bomb that, had he known it, was due to go off with a great deal of panache and quite astounding consequences.

Blissfully unaware of what he was doing, Lewis kept his hand over the lamp and felt Casimir's presence drain out of him.

"Goodbye, Lewis," Casimir said from inside the lamp. "Don't forget, the invisibility spell will wear off quite soon! You'd better hurry back to your seat!"

22. The Hole in the Wall

In the depths of the Underground City, the clouds of stifling, choking dust raised by the explosion had reduced visibility to zero and all Murdo, Wullie and Tammy Souter could do was head in the general direction of the blast and hope for the best. Coughing and spluttering, they ran, hands outstretched towards the vault.

Tammy, as it happened, had done his work well. The side of the vault had been torn open and as they stepped through the massive hole they stopped and, peering uncertainly through the swirling clouds of dust, looked with awe at what had once been shelf upon shelf of neatly stacked banknotes. They were neat no longer for the shelving that had held them was hanging off the walls at all angles and the place was littered with pile upon pile of notes that had flown everywhere with the force of the explosion.

"There must be millions here!" Murdo gasped, his eyes darting round the vault greedily. "Come on, boys, help yourselves!" Pulling thick bin liners out of their pockets they started to pile the money in and, had everything gone to plan, would have made quite a tidy haul and a considerable dent in the finances of the bank.

The Chief Constable's hurried phone call, however, had paid dividends and even as the noise of the blast echoed through the tunnels, a stream of

police cars zoomed up the Mound, sirens blaring.
They came to a screeching halt outside the imposing premises of the Bank of Scotland and passers-
by looked on in amazement as dozens of policemen
tumbled out of the cars and headed for the front
door; a door held invitingly open for them by their
own Chief Constable.

"There was an explosion a few minutes ago,"
he said briefly to the Chief Inspector who headed
the operation. "The bank's security staff are just
opening the vault up now."

"Good, with any luck we'll catch them red-
handed," answered the Chief Inspector as he and
his men raced for the stairs.

Murdo and Wullie heard the sound of the vault
door being opened and acted quickly. "The police!"
said Wullie, totally flabbergasted. "How come they
got here so quick?"

"Come on," Murdo said. "Grab what you can!"
So saying, he piled a few more armfuls of notes into
his bags and hefting them over his shoulder, stumbled towards the hole in the wall. Tammy Souter
followed close on his heels and together they took
the steep slope of the little alley at a run.

Although they naturally assumed that Wullie
would be following them, this did not actually
happen, for Wullie, in his headlong flight from
the ghosts, had managed to rip the side off one of
his trainers and, in turning to follow the others,
had stood on a loose shoelace. Not unnaturally, he
tripped over his feet and in a spectacular effort
to keep his balance, grabbed at some shelving.
Several things then happened in quick succession.

Firstly, the shelving fell off the wall; secondly, it knocked him unconscious and, thirdly, as a grand finale, countless bundles of banknotes cascaded downwards in slithering waves to bury him under a tidy pile that, at a vague estimate, could be reckoned in millions.

So it was, that the hoards of policemen and bank security men who barged through the vault door in a rush, did not actually notice Wullie, buried as he was under a fortune in banknotes. Naturally assuming that the crooks had flown, they made straight for the hole in the wall and then slowed in amazement as the light of their torches revealed the dark, secret alleys of the Underground City. It took their breath away almost literally for not only did the vision of the old, deserted houses stop them in their tracks but the alley was still full of heavy clouds of dust that swirled eerily in the draught from the open vault. They looked at one another in apprehension as fear curdled their stomachs. No horror movie could have had a more spine-chilling opening. It looked a ghastly, awful place.

"Come on, let's go!" choked the Chief Inspector, flashing his torch up the steep little alley that rose in front of them. "Sir Archie said they'd be in here somewhere!"

The policemen scrambled up the alley but, as they reached the top, came to a stumbling halt as they met a sight that would have made the bravest man quail; for they were just in time to meet the army of furious ghosts that were out to get Murdo and could only gape in horror as the host of weird, horrible figures swooped down the alleyway towards them.

The sudden appearance of the ghosts stopped the policemen in their tracks; their faces white and set. Never, in their lives, had they imagined anything like this. Talk about a nightmare gone wrong. Their torches shone right through the phantoms as they came at them from all angles — even through the walls! Accustomed as they were to facing up to hardened criminals on a daily basis, no one could accuse the police of cowardice but this … this was definitely something else. They clutched at one another in sheer terror and backed down the alley as the wailing, moaning, screaming ghosts descended on them.

Murdo heard the noise and grinned. "That's given the police something to think about!" he said gleefully. "Come on, we're nearly there!"

"Nearly where, Murdo?" groaned Tammy Souter who was gasping for breath. Exercise had never been his strong point and he was regretting it now.

"We're going to see the pantomime," Murdo said.

"We're *what?*" Tammy Souter couldn't believe his ears. "You're having me on!"

"You'll enjoy it," Murdo grinned. *"Ali Baba and the Forty Thieves!"*

Tammy muttered something unprintable and it was then that Murdo noticed that there were only two of them.

"Hang on a minute!" he said. "Where's Wullie?"

They stopped and, breathing heavily, looked back down the eerie stretch of old houses that lined the narrow street. There was nothing and nobody there.

"We can't go back for him," Tammy muttered, looking at Murdo pleadingly. "We'll run straight into the police if we do. *And* the ghosts!"

Murdo pressed his lips together. He knew that Tammy was right but Wullie was his buddy and he didn't want to see him in Saughton Prison.

"They'll have nicked him by now," Tammy said. "Bound to have."

"Aye, I suppose you're right," Murdo agreed, bitterness welling up inside him.

"Poor old Wullie," Tammy Souter eyed him sideways. "Thick as two short planks but a good sort."

As the sound of running feet echoed along the tunnel, Murdo moved quickly. "They're onto us," he hissed. "Up those steps, quick, and do as I tell you or *we'll* be for the chop as well!"

The cellars of the Assembly Hall were empty as Murdo and Tammy, sweating under the weight of the bags they carried, made their way up yet another flight of stairs. Tammy's eyes rounded in wonder as he saw the stacks of costumes, scenery and props that filled the place. Murdo hadn't been joking when he'd mentioned the pantomime!

A quick glance down a corridor told Murdo all he wanted to know. The door between the stage and the audience was locked and a burly security man was on guard. He ran downstairs again to where Tammy waited. "Dump the bags over in that corner and put on one of those costumes. Quick now, fast as you can!"

Murdo pulled a pair of baggy satin trousers over his jeans and added a matching tunic that hid his sweater. "Put your socks and shoes in your pocket, Tammy. We can't leave anything behind!"

"I look a sight!" Tammy muttered. "And what about the cash? We can't just leave it here. Somebody's sure to nick it!"

"These laundry baskets look just the thing," Murdo said, pointing to half a dozen tall, straw baskets. "Put the bags in them. If anyone looks in they'll think it's dirty washing! With any luck we can collect them later!"

Leaving the cellars, they strode purposefully towards the stage and were horrified when a little old woman grabbed at them. "You've ruined your make-up," she scolded, peering up at the streaks of dirt on their faces. "Where on earth have you been to get your faces so dirty?" Murdo and Tammy looked at one another warily as the woman made an exasperated noise. "Come in here this minute! How could you ever think of going on stage with your make-up in that state! Really!"

It was fortunate for both Tammy and Murdo that by the time she had finished with them, they were more or less completely unrecognizable for, as she shepherded them towards the extras, milling in the wings for the next crowd scene, several policemen emerged from the cellars and looked around, completely thunderstruck at having landed bang in the middle of a pantomime!

Murdo managed to keep a straight face as they mingled with the rest of the exotically attired cast but his mind was in turmoil. How had the police

got onto them so quickly? Could Wullie have ratted
on them?

It hadn't been Wullie who had ratted on them,
however. Wullie was still in dreamland under a fortune in used banknotes. No, it had been the ghosts
that had given the game away, for Mary King had
remembered Neil's words and, to this day, the
policemen present remember the look on their
Chief Inspector's face when Mary King had sailed
into view and halted the rampaging ghosts.

"My good man," she'd said imperiously. The
Chief Inspector's jaw had dropped in amazement
and he'd straightened instinctively for, despite a
difference of at least five centuries, he realized
that he was being addressed by the equivalent of
a Morningside lady of good family and a proper
tartar at that. "My good man," she continued,
"we are just as anxious as you are to find the people who did this. We will help you all we can. My
friends here," she indicated the ghosts, "will show
you where they might be hiding!"

The astounded policemen looked at their Chief
Inspector in total amazement as he nodded and
so it was that, five minutes later, a large, totally
gob-smacked slice of the Edinburgh Constabulary
found itself fanning out through the tunnels and
alleys of the Underground City with ghosts as
guides. The Chief Inspector gulped, hoped he'd
done the right thing and, preferring not to think
of what he was going to write in his report, set
off with the old Codger leading the way, along a
narrow street that apparently led to the Assembly
Hall.

"That's got rid of them," Mary King said thankfully as she and the remaining ghosts watched the last of the policemen disappear. "Come now," she said, looking at their fearful faces, "they're probably still sealed up but we've got to be sure, haven't we?"

The cellars of the Plague People, as she had told Murdo, were close by but although they had little more to do than walk round a corner, the ghosts eyed one another sideways and moved with a strange reluctance. As it happened, they heard them before they saw them and were seized by a sudden dread as the faint bubbling, moaning noise that seeped through the walls into the alley seemed to grow louder as they approached. Clarinda gave a shriek of fear and Mr Rafferty clapped a hand over his mouth in horror — for the blast of the explosion had not only blown open the vault, it had drastically weakened the sides of the houses. Their walls were bulging, weak and crumbling and they gaped in horror as, poking out from amid the streams of dust trickling down into the alley, they could see long, white fingers groping frantically through the cracks in the stone-work, picking and poking away desperately, trying to get out.

The Plague People! There was no doubt about it! There was nothing they could do to stop them! They would surely soon be free! Suddenly a long, thin, pasty-white arm crept through a slit in the wall and groped at the air with long, crooked fingers.

It was enough! The ghosts fled in terror!

23. Goblin Market

As Murdo and Tammy mingled with the crowd onstage, they gradually relaxed. Dressed as they were, they had managed to blend in quite well and if they kept their heads down, Murdo reckoned, then they might well get away with it. He winked at Tammy. No one, so far, had accosted them and although they both kept a wary eye on the increasing numbers of policemen that prowled the wings they were soon caught up in the action of the plot as Ali Baba attempted to rescue his beloved Morgana from among the exotically dressed slave-girls who were being paraded in the market before the tall, impressive figure of the Sultan.

Nevertheless, they almost jumped out of their skins when two huge, green monsters suddenly erupted from a tall, gold-framed mirror that stood nearby. It was only when the rest of the crowd shied away in fright that they realized that this wasn't part of the act, for the wave of fear that rippled through the cast was genuine. Everyone stared in horror at the dreadful creatures, absolutely dumbfounded.

The Stage Manager clapped a hand dramatically to his forehead. "Where on earth did they spring from?" he hissed, furiously. *"They're* not in the script!"

"What *are* they?" demanded the Chief Inspector who had been standing at his elbow, scanning the stage for familiar faces. He looked at the monstrous things in disbelief and saw problems looming. The ghosts were bad enough — but monsters as well! His heart sank. They were *never* going to believe him back at the station!

Matt Lafferty whirled round as the goblins landed with a thump in the middle of the stage, his nose instinctively wrinkling in disgust as the most awful pong hit his nostrils. "Help ma' bob!" he muttered, totally astounded. He lowered his staff as if to protect the Sultan but could only stare at them in horror for the creatures that had appeared out of nowhere were not only unknown to science, but were also repulsive, stank to the heavens and looked totally ferocious!

Neil and Clara recognized the goblins immediately. So did Lewis, who remembered them from his trip to Ardray. Sir James, too, sat looking totally appalled for he had been responsible for them being in the mirror in the first place. He'd whopped them over the head and chucked them into the mirror the previous year when he'd been trying to get the Sultan's crown back from Prince Kalman and had certainly never expected to see them again.

The goblins got rather shakily to their feet and peered around, blinded by the stage lights. They were bigger than the average man, a horrid, sickly, green colour with skin that looped in dry, knobbly folds over their bodies. Their eyes were red and savage and their hands and feet ended in huge, sharp claws that were even now opening and closing as they eyed the people round about as though wondering which of them they were going to attack first. The stench was indescribable and yet nobody ran off the stage. Everyone stared, held in a terrible thrall of horror as they watched the creatures grunt and slobber dreadfully from mouths that showed fearsome sets of wickedly curved teeth.

Neil and Clara looked at one another and, with sinking hearts, realized that they were the only ones in a position to do anything. Neil knew, too, that they'd have to try and kill the goblins for there was no way they could let them attack the cast. Their fearsome claws would tear people apart and they wouldn't stop. They'd attack everyone and everything on stage.

Like the Grand Vizier, Neil turned the staff he was carrying into a spear and gestured to Clara to do the same. The ornamental point was, he knew, made from steel and they'd both had to be careful whilst carrying them for fear of doing someone an injury. "We've got to kill them," he hissed at her.

"Kill them?" Matt Lafferty heard him quite plainly and was horrified. "Are you nuts, or something!" he whispered, totally shaken. "You can't *kill* people in the middle of a *pantomime!* The place is loaded with kids!"

Neil, his face set and determined, looked him in the eye. "We have to," he replied. "These things aren't people wearing costumes, they're goblins! And ... and actually, I think you'll have to do the killing, Mr Lafferty," he said. "Clara and I don't have the strength but if we keep one of the goblins occupied, you could spear the other one!"

Matt Lafferty looked over at the two goblins who, recovering from the shock of being so suddenly ejected from the mirror, were making horrible noises and baring their claws and teeth at the crowd. It was the slavering mouths and the gut-wrenching stink of them that finally convinced him that the goblins were for real and, as he nodded to Neil, the jovial comedian of the pantomime, despite his turban, changed into a warrior straight from the film of *Braveheart*.

The goblins, meanwhile, had spotted the long table at the side of the stage that had been laid out for the village feast. The roast pig, turkeys, haunches of venison and great hams that the Ranger had made with such care, were actually all made of papier-mâché but they looked real and inviting and, as the goblins lumbered gruntingly towards them, arms outstretched hungrily, Neil and Clara ran in front of the table and held them off with their spears while the Grand Vizier made his approach from the rear.

Totally horrified at what was going on, Sir James made to rise from his seat and head backstage when there was a sudden flash, a puff of smoke and a crack of sound that sent the goblins jumping warily backwards. They knew immediately what it meant. It meant that a wizard of some sort had arrived and they stared around to see who, what and where, he was.

Sir James also knew what the crack of sound portended and, scanning the stage swiftly, felt a sense of disappointment creep over him as he saw that no one had appeared and nothing seemed to have changed. Then he noticed Matt Lafferty staring at the Sultan and as he, too, looked at the stately figure on the throne, noticed a subtle difference in him. The Sultan of the pantomime was a tall, thin man and although the clothes were the same, this was by no means the same person. He was heavier and bulkier and as he turned to look into the audience, Sir James sat back in his seat with a sigh of relief, as he recognized the stern, dark face beneath the turban. He relaxed thankfully; the Ranger had obviously got to the hill in time and told his story. The Sultan was indeed a Sultan. Their Sultan; Sulaiman the Red.

From then on, the Sultan took charge. As the goblins rushed towards Neil and Clara, he stood up, stretched out his arm and, as an astounded cast watched in amazement, a beam of light crackled towards the goblins. The goblins gave frightful shrieks as the hexes struck home and they disappeared in two puffs of vile, green smoke. Neil and Clara, still holding their spears at the ready, looked at the Sultan blankly but as he beckoned them back to the dais they met his eyes and almost laughed with relief. The Sultan had arrived! Everything would be all right now!

The audience had been quick to react to the uncertainty on stage and Sir James could feel the rustle of unease that permeated the theatre. He started to clap loudly and as people half-heartedly joined in, the Sultan bowed low and sent another spell sweeping over the audience. It was a warm, comfortable, reassuring spell that took everyone back to the days of their childhood and the magical thrill of the theatre.

As the spell took hold, the clapping became a positive storm of applause and when the pantomime reverted to its original script, everyone settled back happily to enjoy it.

Sulaiman the Red, however, still sat on the throne, overseeing the proceedings with a wary eye. Given the fact that the magic mirror was still on, he was ready for surprises but even he had no idea that Prince Casimir was curled, worried and uncomfortable, inside the magic lamp. Casimir had watched the Sultan hex the goblins and was both disappointed and fearful. Fearful because the Sultan was there at all and disappointed beyond belief because the mirror had not, after all, held his son.

Lewis sat in his seat, absolutely stunned. What on earth was going on? He tried to remember what Casimir had told him about the MacArthurs and the Sultan's crown but it was all rather mixed up in his mind. He knew, though, that what he had just observed was no stage trick. The Sultan had used magic to make the goblins disappear and surely, he thought, the Sultan in the first act had been thinner?

From then on he sat quivering in his seat knowing that although Casimir had left him, the world of magic still had a few tricks up its sleeve and that perhaps some of them had yet to be played. In this he was quite correct for, as the pantomime progressed, it suddenly dawned on Lewis that the magic lamp, into which he'd so casually deposited Casimir, was actually going to be used and, indeed, seemed to have an important part to play in the plot. And his heart sank as he realized what it would be …

On stage, a relaxed Clara had recovered from the shock of the goblins and was now following the action with amusement. The scene that was coming next, where Ali Baba rubs the lamp and the genie appears, was her favourite part of the show. She was well aware that Alec Johnston was already in place behind a huge pottery jar that stood near her. He was busy hooking the ends of his blue, silk cloak over his fingers so that it would flare out as he made his fabulous leap in front of Ali Baba, when he rubbed the lamp. Eyes sparkling with anticipation, she watched as Ali Baba wandered over to one of the stalls and looked casually at the lamp.

Lewis cringed in his seat and Casimir almost had a heart attack. Surely not, he thought. It couldn't be. Someone was picking up the lamp!

"Only five piastres, effendi!" the stall-keeper urged brightly, holding out the lamp for Ali Baba to see.

"Five piastres!" Ali Baba repeated in mock horror. "It's not new! In fact it's just a battered, old bit of scrap. I'll give you two piastres for it!"

"Three, effendi," the stall-keeper pleaded. "Three and it's yours!"

Ali Baba fished in his pockets and threw three coins down on the stall. "It's a deal," he said, taking the lamp and holding it up, "but you might have given it a bit of a polish before you tried to sell it," he grumbled, breathing on it and rubbing it with his sleeve.

Although the audience had been ready for a bang of some sort they hadn't reckoned on the roar of sound that resounded throughout the Assembly Hall. They almost leapt from their seats and those on stage jerked backwards, watching in alarmed fascination as a huge puff of smoke spiralled upwards in billowing clouds from the narrow mouth of the lamp. It swirled fantastically and gradually took both shape and form. And there he was, thought Lewis. Old Casimir, himself! The genie of the lamp. And he was absolutely breathtaking!

At much the same time, Alec Johnston had made his less than spectacular entrance; leaping forward, his cloak billowing out nicely behind him, to land at Ali Baba's feet.

To tell you the truth, nobody much noticed him; for all eyes were fixed on Casimir who, amid billowing clouds of smoke, was now ten feet tall and growing!

24. The Plague People

Underneath the theatre, in the lanes and alleys of the Underground City, the Plague People had steadily picked their way free and were now roaming the streets at will. The walls that had held them prisoner had crumbled under the pressure of their desperate attempts for freedom and as they sallied triumphantly forth, their wailing cries struck fear into the hearts of those who heard them.

The police were still in the Underground City at the time, some in the vaults of the bank, while others searched methodically through the streets and houses for traces of Murdo, Wullie and Tammy Souter.

The ghosts guided them here and there and it hadn't take the policemen long to appreciate their help; for without them, they'd soon have been lost in the labyrinth of alleys and streets that seemed to stretch all the way down the High Street to Holyrood. Surprisingly enough, they worked quite well together. The ghosts were all right, thought the policemen, as long as you didn't look too closely at their awful eyes.

Then they heard it in the distance, a strange moaning, bubbling noise that echoed weirdly among the houses. They stopped instinctively, flashing their torches back down the alleys and seeing nothing, looked sharply at the ghosts.

"What's that awful racket?" a constable asked apprehensively and took no comfort from the sudden expressions of fear that appeared on the ghosts' faces. They, themselves, it seemed, were suddenly scared to death and were looking down the narrow streets in terror. "The Plague People!" they whispered.

Moments later, they came into view.

Ghosts and policemen alike gasped in horror for the ghosts of the plague were, indeed, the stuff of nightmares. Dressed in long, white, hooded robes that drifted into mist, their pale faces were mottled black with boils and their long skinny arms stretched out hungrily as they swung swiftly and silently between the houses searching for their prey.

"Run," the ghosts snapped. "Follow us. We know all the short cuts. Quickly! Run for your lives!"

The policemen, who had paled at the mention of the plague, did exactly that. Following the ghosts, they dived in and out of houses and alleys, knowing that had Mary King not made her offer of help, they wouldn't have stood a chance and would soon have been caught by the nameless horrors that chased them. As it was, they reached the stair up to the Assembly Hall with the terrifying apparitions not far behind and it was only when the last policeman scrambled white-faced to safety that the cellar door was slammed shut and firmly locked.

The same thing happened in the bank. The bank security staff took one look at the drifting horrors that were sloping down the alley towards them and raced for the safety of the bank's interior. It was a close run thing, for even as the ghosts sailed towards them over the scattered piles of banknotes, they were still hefting the door of the vault shut, with no thought for the money left abandoned and unguarded in its shattered ruins.

"MacArthur! Lord Rothlan!" Jaikie said, springing to his feet in alarm for the second time that evening. The first scare, when the goblins had shot out of the magic mirror, had been bad enough but this was worse. Much worse! "Will you come and look at this!" he said, gesturing towards the crystal ball. "The Plague People are loose!"

Kitor gave a squawk of alarm and Arthur heaved himself to his feet so that he, too, could see what was going on. Lord Rothlan and the MacArthur hastily rose to their feet and strode towards the glowing crystal on its ornate stand. It showed a ghastly, horrible scene as its eye followed the ghosts of the Plague People as they glided with swift, hungry eagerness along the alleys of the Underground City.

Lady Ellan, too, peered into the crystal, her nose wrinkling in disgust. A nameless fear made her shiver. "They really look awful, don't they!" she whispered. "But how on earth did they get out? I thought their cellars had been sealed up?"

"It must have been yon bank robbers that Neil was telling me about," muttered the MacArthur. "He said they were trying to break into the vaults of the Bank of Scotland."

"Do you think they broke into their cellars instead?" Jaikie whispered.

"Whatever they did, they certainly got more than they bargained for." Lord Rothlan looked and sounded worried as he eyed the hooded white shapes with their bloated, mottled faces.

"You ... you don't think Neil and Clara might be down there, do you?" Jaikie interrupted fearfully.

Lady Ellan shook her head. "I shouldn't think so," she said. "They're in the pantomime."

"Let's see if we can get hold of Sir Archie ..." Lord Rothlan said. "Can you find him for me, Jaikie?"

The crystal dimmed and then brightened to show the interior of the bank where white-faced security staff clutched at one another, shivering at the memory of the ghastly drifting shapes that had so nearly caught them.

"Well, it certainly looks as though something's been happening there," the MacArthur commented as the crystal scanned the bank's marble foyer.

"Look, there's Sir Archie," Jaikie pointed to the door of the bank where the Chief Constable was talking busily to Jock MacPherson.

"Thank goodness he's all right," the MacArthur muttered and, as the crystal reverted once more to the ghost-ridden streets of the Underground City, he rubbed his chin thoughtfully. "Mind you, it'll be interesting to see what he plans to do about that little lot," he mused.

"Do? With the Plague People?" Lord Rothlan said, looking up with a frown. "There isn't much he *can* do, is there?"

"There's not a lot *we* can do either, come to that," Lady Ellan remarked, slipping her hand through her husband's arm.

"Well, it looks as though he might be coming here in a minute," Jaikie interrupted as the crystal dimmed and brightened once more. "He's just left the bank and called his carpet!"

Instinctively, they all turned to look at the side of the cave where a magic carpet had unrolled itself gently and was already whisking its way towards one of the tunnels that led to the surface of Arthur's Seat.

The MacArthur eyed it sourly. "Aye," he said as it disappeared into the gloom, "and when he arrives, I'll bet you a pound for a penny that he thinks I can get rid of the Plague People with a hex! Just like that!"

"You can't really blame him," Lord Rothlan smiled wryly. "He won't understand that we're powerless to help."

A few minutes later, they looked up as a carpet carrying the Chief Constable sailed into the huge cavern from one of the tunnels.

"Here he is now," Lady Ellan said as the carpet flew towards them.

The Chief Constable greeted the MacArthur and then seeing Lord Rothlan, strode over to congratulate him on his marriage. "Lord Rothlan!" Sir Archie shook hands with him warmly, "and Lady Ellan," he said delightedly. "My warmest congratulations to you both!" He cleared his throat. "MacArthur," he said, "can I ask you about the ghosts in Mary King's Close?"

The MacArthur looked at Lord Rothlan and sighed. "I know you'd like me to help, but ..."

"It's serious, MacArthur," Sir Archie interrupted urgently. "The ghosts of the plague victims have escaped. Mary King told me just five minutes ago. She managed to get all of my men out safely, but according to her the Plague People have taken over the whole Underground City!"

The MacArthur sighed. "I know what you're thinking," he said, "but I can't do it! I can't hex them away!"

The Chief Constable looked horrified as his eyes flew from one serious face to another.

"Ghosts aren't magic people, you see," Rothlan explained. "They are spirits of the dead and our magic doesn't affect them."

"I'm afraid it's something that the ghosts have to sort out for themselves," the MacArthur said.

"But the plague!" The Chief Constable was astounded. "You've got to help! Once they get into the streets there'll be panic! To say nothing of an epidemic of the Black Death in Edinburgh!"

"Aye, you'll have to keep them confined to the Underground City," agreed the MacArthur. "No doubt about it! All the exits and entrances will have to be sealed up so the plague ghosts can't get out into the streets! You do realize that they need actual openings to get through, don't you?"

The Chief Constable looked at him in relief. "You mean they can't drift through walls and doors like Mary King's lot?"

"That power was taken away from them by the Council of Elders," the MacArthur explained, "otherwise how would the closed cellars have held them prisoner for all these years?"

"I see." the Chief Constable said grimly. "Well, then, it's not as bad as I thought, but it's bad enough! It'll only take one of them to get out and the whole of Edinburgh will be in a panic! Murdo Fraser's got to be found! And found quickly!"

25. The Genie of the Lamp

Matt Lafferty, the magnificently-clad Grand Vizier, got such a shock at Casimir's sudden, dramatic appearance that he almost leapt the height of himself. He gawped in wonder and backed somewhat nervously away — for the towering genie was a frightening sight, his face grim amid the swirling clouds of multi-coloured smoke that billowed round him. He grabbed Neil and Clara and, pulling them towards the Sultan's throne, let out a muttered stream of broad Scots that fortunately, given the circumstances, few people understood.

Casimir, now at least twenty feet tall, reared from the spout of the little lamp, smoke eddying around him in clouds. He was furiously angry! Angry with Lewis for being idiotic enough to put him in the lamp in the first place, and with Ali Baba for having been fool enough to actually rub the lamp in the second.

Alec Johnston was also furious. He knew that during rehearsals he had made a lot of enemies — jealous, no doubt, at his fantastic performance — and being totally self-centred, didn't for one second believe that Casimir was real. And who could blame him? Genies, after all, only exist in story books! So it wasn't entirely his fault that he thought someone was taking the mickey with a vengeance. He'd no idea how they'd managed it but they'd stolen his thunder, ruined his act and

made him look a fool; for he gloried in the knowledge that his magnificent entrance was the star
moment of the pantomime.

Spitting with fury, he reached out, grabbed
the magic lamp from Ali Baba and threw it with
all the strength he could muster, into the wings.
Seeing it coming, a policeman ducked swiftly but
the monstrous slave-merchant standing behind
him, wasn't quite so quick off the mark and the
lamp hit him full in the face with considerable
force.

Now the slave-merchant, who in the past had
been the butt of quite a few of Alec Johnston's
more snide remarks, positively hated the strut-
ting, trumped-up star. When the lamp fell to the
floor and he saw who had thrown it, he was not
at all amused. A red rage seized hold of him and
with a roar of fury he drew his scimitar and, blood
streaming down his face from a badly mangled
nose, charged onto the stage.

The genie saw him coming and turned quite pale
as the mountainous man thundered through the
wings towards him. He leapt back and, grabbing
a scimitar from the ranks of the Sultan's Guard,
prepared for battle. Heartened by the knowledge
that the slave-merchant was no swordsman, he
leapt at him bravely enough and, scimitars clash-
ing angrily, they fought their way several times
round the stage, into the wings and back again.
The Stage Manager, white-faced and horrified,
looked close to a nervous breakdown by this time
but nobody dared stop the two men who were
fighting with deadly passion and deadlier weapons

— for the way things were, neither could give way to the other without one of them being beheaded!

Casimir, suddenly deprived of his home in the lamp, had promptly shrunk in size and was now the rather sour, cross old man that Lewis knew so well. He didn't even see the genie and the slave-merchant fighting around him but only had eyes for the Sultan. As their eyes met, there was a brief clash of wills, Casimir, however, had had all the time in the world to ponder his behaviour when he'd been held captive in the well at Al Antara. He was a changed man and, although puzzled at his sudden passion to own the crown, he had no wish to confront Sulaiman the Red. So, he did the only thing he could under the circumstances. He bowed low to the Sultan who rose to his feet and beckoned him forward.

Neil and Clara, standing on each side of the dais, looked at one another in amazement. "Prince Casimir," Neil mouthed to Clara, who nodded in agreement for the resemblance between father and son was strong. Knowing the depth of the enmity that existed between the two men, they watched in fascination as the Sultan extended his hand to be kissed; the huge, ruby ring on his finger glowing in the spotlights. Casimir looked the Sultan in the eyes and then knelt before him and kissed his ring. It was a historic occasion in the world of magic. Sir James sat tense with excitement in his seat as he realized its importance and even Matt Lafferty was astute enough to know that this was not acting.

His eyes goggled as, out of the blue, an ornate chair appeared on the dais to the right of the

Sultan's throne. Not quite as grand or as large as the Sultan's but imposing nevertheless. The Sultan rose and taking Casimir's hand, sat him graciously beside him.

It was only when the genie and the slave-merchant passed again in furious combat that the Sultan seemed to realize that there was a battle going on under his nose. As the men headed for the wings, he lifted his arm and as he did so, both scimitars suddenly flew into the air and the two men collapsed onto the stage.

The Stage Manager was close to tears. Now what? Would nothing in this pantomime go right? He was furious with Alec Johnston and also quite convinced that by this time the audience, having completely lost the plot, would get up and go home. Worse, however, was to come!

Ever since the magic mirror had disgorged the two goblins onto the stage, Sir James had been waiting for another figure to emerge from its depths. So, to a certain extent, had Neil and Clara, for they, too, had been present on that last terrible day at Ardray when Prince Kalman, in an attempt to escape, had been trapped between mirrors.

The Sultan, however, was most certainly expecting his arrival and when, like the goblins, a somewhat dishevelled Prince Kalman was suddenly catapulted out of the mirror into the middle of the stage, he merely waved his hand and a spell transformed him into a gorgeously-robed Turkish prince.

Sir James clapped furiously, the audience did likewise and a rather stunned Prince Kalman

bowed with regal grace and then gawped in a
most un-princely fashion at the sight of his own
father sitting at the right-hand side of the Turkish
Sultan, Sulaiman the Red. The look of relief that
crossed his face when he realized that his father
was alive was, however, fleeting. His brain, working with the speed of light, swiftly told him that
the Sultan must not only have held him prisoner
for countless years but also seemed to have suc-
ceeded in making him his vassal. Memories of that
last, dreadful scene at Ardray, when the Sultan
had taken his crown back, were still fresh in his
mind and as his anger boiled anew, he glared furiously at the Sultan.

The Grand Vizier who, by this time, was now
positively thriving on the totally unexpected,
nipped smartly out of the way as another chair
materialized beside the Sultan's throne. He hadn't
a clue what was happening but as every theatrical instinct in his body was geared to keeping the
show going at all costs, he stepped forward with
a flourish, bowed deeply to the young prince and
escorted him to the dais.

The Sultan rose from his throne, held his hands
out in welcome and gestured to the empty chair
beside him.

In the audience, Sir James sat rigid and hastily
breathed a silent prayer for, in a matter of seconds, Prince Kalman's expression had changed
from blank astonishment to blind fury. Neil and
Clara, standing like statues on either side of the
dais, hoped fervently that he wouldn't recognize
them and turned their heads away slightly while

Casimir, who wanted more than anything to hug his son, gripped the arms of his chair in anxiety but did not dare intervene. Such was the crackling tension in the atmosphere that even the Grand Vizier stepped back, his eyes looking warily from Prince Kalman to the Sultan and back again. Indeed, Kalman's arrogance in the face of the Sultan's power was nothing short of mind-boggling. The Sultan could have hexed him there and then but Kalman was consumed by a black rage that made him fearless.

"How can you sit there, father?" he snarled. "The vassal of Sulaiman the Red!"

Casimir made to rise but the Sultan stepped forward. "Come Prince Kalman," he said sincerely. "You are as welcome as your father to my court. Let there be peace among us as there was in times long gone."

"Never!" Kalman almost spat the word out. His blue eyes blazed in fury as his glance swept the scene — and rested inevitably on Neil and Clara.

That did it. The Sultan knew it, Sir James knew it and so did Casimir although he hadn't a clue as to why the sight of two children should send his son through the roof in a towering rage.

There was, in fact, nothing that could have been better designed to send Kalman's temper rocketing skywards than the sight of Neil and Clara. *"You!"* the prince snarled, with a ferocity that sent the Grand Vizier's eyebrows snapping together in alarm. "So *you* are here as well, are you?" he hissed, venomously. "Many's the time I've longed to have *you* in my power!" Clara wilted under the unrelieved fury of his gaze and as Neil stepped forward to protect her, Kalman grabbed each of their arms and, muttering the words of a hex under his breath, the three of them vanished in a cloud of smoke.

Casimir leapt from his chair, screaming in horror as his son disappeared; the Sultan, hiding his fury, pursed his lips impassively; Sir James looked thunderstruck and tears sprang to Lewis's eyes. He knew how badly Casimir had wanted to find his son and now look what had happened!

As Casimir wailed and wept, the Sultan looked round and decided that as far as he was concerned, the pantomime had more than served its purpose. He met Matt Lafferty's sharp, brown eyes with a glint of amused appreciation in his troubled smile, lifted his arm and cast a spell that not only replaced his own undoubted majesty with the body of the original Sultan, but also brought the pantomime back to the point when the genie appeared.

So, once again, Alec Johnston made his magnificent leap onto the stage. This time there was no Casimir to spoil it and the applause was deafening. It was only the Grand Vizier, Lewis and Sir James who noticed that neither Neil nor Clara stood guard at either side of the Sultan's throne.

26. Smoking Kills

Murdo and Tammy Souter didn't stand a chance.

A black beetle couldn't have left the Assembly Hall that night without being thoroughly scrutinized! There were policemen everywhere and it wasn't at all surprising that Murdo and Tammy were caught fair and square when they tried to leave the theatre with the audience.

After Prince Kalman's sudden disappearance, the pantomime had suffered no more untoward interruptions, much to the relief of Sir James, Matt Lafferty, Lewis and the Stage Manager. The finale was a triumph and the applause had been rapturous.

After many curtain calls had been taken, Sir James had gone on stage and given a short but witty speech, reminding the audience that, as the performance was for charity, he hoped that each and every one of them would contribute generously. There were baskets, he said, in the foyer for their donations which would all be given to Children's Aid, a worthwhile cause if ever there was one.

The mention of baskets had, at the time, filled both Murdo and Tammy with apprehension and sadly for them, their fears were not unfounded, for as they tried to escape the searching eyes of the policemen scattered round the foyer, they saw many people putting cheques and cash in the same tall, Ali Baba baskets that held the takings of their robbery. As there wasn't a lot they could do about it, they gritted their teeth as they headed for the swing doors that they hoped would lead to freedom.

It was not to be, however, for Sir Archie's instructions had been brief, simple and to the point — and it must be admitted that the hand of the law, when it finally fell on their shoulders, was not totally unexpected.

As Murdo had said, it was a fair cop and they'd gone quietly. But when he got to the police station and found that Wullie hadn't been arrested, he'd really started to worry. With sickening clarity, he'd remembered the arrival of white-faced policemen backstage and although they'd been tight-lipped about what had gone on in the Underground City, he had a sneaking suspicion that perhaps it wasn't only the ghosts that had scared them. Perhaps the Plague People *had* got out? Mary King had warned him. What if they'd got out and found Wullie? Such an innocent! Such a daft idiot! And so scared of the ghosts!

Murdo hammered violently on the door of his cell. "I want to see the Chief Inspector," he roared through the grill, "and I want to see him *now!*"

The constable who unlocked his cell door looked at him with more than a touch of awe, wondering what on earth Murdo had been up to this time. "You're in luck, Murdo," he said, eyeing him strangely, "but it's no' the Chief Inspector that wants to see you! It's the Chief Constable himself!"

Murdo blinked, startled. "Sir Archie?"

The constable grinned. "Aye, Murdo! Sir Archie, himself! You've made it to the top this time!"

Inside the hill, Jaikie, who was checking to see if any of the plague ghosts had managed to escape into the High Street, sat up suddenly for the third time that evening. "Didn't Sir Archie say they'd got everyone out of the Underground City?" he queried.

"Yes," the MacArthur looked up in surprise, "that's what he told us, anyway."

"Well, he was wrong! Come over here and have a look! There's still someone in there," Jaikie said.

"It's not a policeman, though!" Hamish muttered, peering over his shoulder.

The MacArthur and Rothlan got up and moved over to the crystal.

"It must be one of the bank robbers," Jaikie said. And they watched in horror as the plague ghosts homed in on the lonely figure.

It *was* one of the bank robbers! It was Wullie!

When Wullie woke up under a veritable fortune in used banknotes, he had a head on him fit to burst. At best, it felt as though he'd been hit by a couple of hundred hammers. As this pain-filled daze lasted for some time, it was a while before he remembered about the vault and it was only when the realization slowly dawned that he must still be in the bank that he tentatively opened his eyes and sat up, shedding piles of notes.

It was a mistake. His head swam and his eyes glazed but not before he saw the banknotes

that lay in piles around him. Hundreds of them!
Thousands of them!

Now Wullie was not overly blessed with brains
but his situation would, at that moment, have left
a genius floundering! There he was, in the vault,
all the lights were on, there was money everywhere
and the whole place was as quiet as the grave. Not
another soul anywhere! No police, no bank staff,
nobody at all!

In the dim, cloudy, outer-reaches of his mind,
Wullie wondered about Murdo and this vague rec-
ollection strengthened when he saw his bin-liner
lying beside him, half-full of money — he looked
at it thoughtfully and as he looked, his brain, very
gently, began to tick over. Not very fast, mind you,
but it was a start! The first thing it told him was
that he needed a cigarette. It was a sad fact, but
Wullie couldn't think at all without a cigarette in
his mouth. So he lit up, tried to ignore his pound-
ing head and thought about what he was going to
do.

Now this was important because until then, it
was actually Murdo that had done all the thinking.
Murdo said do this, and he did it! Murdo said go
this way, and he went! Murdo was always there to
see him safely home! Life without Murdo was, in
fact, totally uncharted territory and the only thing
Wullie was quite sure of was that if he wasn't careful, he wouldn't get home. He'd get lost. And that
freaked him out because if he got lost, the ghosts
would get him!

Now, although Wullie's thoughts didn't exactly
move with the speed of light, they were neverthe-

less logical. He lit another cigarette and thought some more. He wasn't sure about the street that went to the Assembly Hall, even though Murdo said they wouldn't have heard the bang from up there. But the bang had been a while ago, surely? This reminded Wullie that he had a watch on. He peered at it through the drum-beats of his thumping headache and saw to his amazement that it had been ages since they'd blown the vault. This cheered him up no end. With a bit of luck, he thought hopefully, the ghosts might, by this time, have gone to bed!

But he made his decision. He wouldn't go near the Assembly Hall. He'd stick to the way he knew. He'd take the old familiar passage to Deacon Brodie's Tavern and get out through their cellars!

Struggling to his feet was a delicate process as every movement jarred his thumping head and sent lights flashing before his eyes. However, he managed it without too much trouble, lit another cigarette and fifteen minutes later was carefully plodding up the steep slope of the little alley, shining his torch over what, to him, was reassuringly familiar ground.

It was when he heard a strange, horrible, gargling sound and saw some white ghosts heading his way down the alley that Jaikie picked him up in the crystal ball.

Now, Wullie hadn't seen these ghosts before and although they didn't look particularly nice, his vision was still desperately blurred from the crack on his head, with the result that the nitty-gritty details of the swooping horrors were totally lost

on him. Murdo, too, had very successfully instilled
the notion into his thick head that the ghosts,
however awful they looked, couldn't do him any
real harm. And as Murdo was always right, the
upshot was that he didn't pay the plague ghosts
a blind bit of notice. This rather stopped them in
their tracks as they weren't used to being ignored
and it made them gurgle and groan even louder as
they swooped around him.

The MacArthur, Rothlan, Ellan and Jaikie all
watched in fascinated horror as Wullie calmly
stopped, lit up again and plodded to the top of the
alley with the ghosts streaming behind him! He
looked around and ahead of him saw the familiar
route to the cellar stretching ahead. Not long now,
thought Wullie!

He noticed, however, that the bubbling, moaning
noises of the ghosts swirling around him seemed to
have subtly changed in tone and now that his head
was feeling slightly better and the cigarettes were
kicking in, looked at them with more attention.
The bubbling noise was now more like a choking,
gargling sound and the awful faces were curling up
frightfully at his cigarette smoke. One ghost was
doubled up in convulsions, another was coughing
fit to burst and a third seemed to be in the process
of complete disintegration!

The MacArthur and Lord Rothlan looked at one
another in startled amazement and Wullie beamed
as realization dawned!

It was his fags!

Now revenge is sweet and Wullie hadn't by
any means forgiven the ghosts for all the shoves,

pushes and icy-cold blasts of the past. He inhaled deeply and blew smoke in their awful faces, watching in delight as they gasped, coughed, choked and more or less creased up. More and more came swinging along the alley and as he lit up again and again, he took them all on quite happily, even waving his arms from time to time so that the fumes of long-standing that lurked in his overcoat wafted towards them and doubled them up in an agony of self-destruction.

It was an unequal battle at best and one that Wullie won, hands down.

"Well!" said the MacArthur, when they had all stopped laughing, "that's certainly solved all Sir Archie's problems, hasn't it?"

"It has that!" Lord Rothlan said, shaking his head in awe as he watched the last of the ghosts fizzle and disappear. "The man deserves a medal!"

Wullie, who hadn't, until then, appreciated the fact that he was a walking weapon of mass destruction, looked round in satisfaction at the empty alley, but it was only when he was convinced that all the ghosts had choked their last that he resumed his journey, a misty figure enveloped in a gauzy haze of cigarette smoke. On reaching the pile of crates that gave onto Deacon Brodie's cellars, he scrambled through the trapdoor and replaced it gently with a sigh of relief. He felt a great sense of achievement. Murdo would be proud of him!

He stopped on the stairs on the way up to the bar and spent quite a while in the Gents, tidying himself up. The shelving had given him a whacking bump but his hair covered most of it and if anyone asked he could always say he'd been in a fight, couldn't he? Not a lot of people ever argued with Wullie, him being over six-feet tall and broad with it, so he wasn't too worried at being asked anything, really. He even stopped to have a quick pint before setting off up the road to his own wee flat on the High Street, well content with his night's work.

The High Street, needless to say, was stiff with police and although they stopped many late-night revellers, checked identities and patted people over for concealed weapons, none of them stopped Wullie.

And it wasn't because he was six-feet tall and broad with it either; it was because the MacArthur and Lord Rothlan reckoned that Wullie deserved to get back to his flat unhindered and, just to make sure, cast a wee spell that quite successfully protected him all the way home!

27. An Uninvited Guest

Lewis couldn't wait to get home. He'd been on tenterhooks ever since Casimir and the Sultan had vanished. Not only Casimir but Prince Kalman and Neil and Clara as well!

Casimir had told him when they'd got home from the ice-rink that Neil and Clara had magic in them but he hadn't really believed it until he'd seen them stand up to the goblins on stage. There was no doubt about it. They'd known who and what the goblins were, all right! He'd expected his parents to make some remark about them at the interval but, like the rest of the audience, they seemed not to have noticed anything amiss. Everything, as far as they were concerned, was totally normal. Magic again, he thought!

After the show, they'd gone backstage and although he'd smiled and chatted with Matt Lafferty and been polite to his father's friend, Sir James, his mind had been elsewhere. He'd liked Sir James, although the understanding twinkle in his eye when he'd said he hoped living in Edinburgh wasn't proving too dull, had been a bit unnerving; almost as if he'd known that he was the Shadow! All he could think of was Casimir and he'd been glad when his parents had eventually said their final goodbyes.

"Well," said his father, putting the car into gear and pulling out into the traffic. "That was quite an evening!"

"It was a super pantomime!" Lewis agreed. "Matt Lafferty was marvellous as the Grand Vizier!"

"Yes," murmured his mother, with a yawn, "the theatre is really quite magical. It takes you into quite a different world, doesn't it?"

"I guess so," Lewis nodded, quite determined to get into the "other world" that very evening! For he still had Casimir's carpet and he was going to use it!

Once in his bedroom, he quickly changed into warmer clothes and as he zipped up his anorak, he looked at the carpet, propped in a corner, against the wall.

Clapping his hands together sharply, he said "carpet," the way Casimir had done. Nothing, however, happened.

"Now listen, carpet," he said seriously as he bent to pick it up, "I know you can hear me, so don't pretend you can't!" He spread the carpet over his bed and looked at it thoughtfully. "Lots of things have happened tonight," he explained, "and I've just *got* to see Casimir! He might be in Arthur's Seat or he might have gone to Ardray but I *have* got to see him. He found his son tonight, that Prince Kalman, and his son didn't want to know him! Would you believe it? After all the time he's spent searching for him?"

The magic carpet wriggled uneasily. "I'm only supposed to carry Prince Casimir," it said.

"Come on, carpet," pleaded Lewis. "Didn't I make you beautiful again when I had my magic wishes?"

"Yes," the carpet breathed, thinking back to the perfectly awful time when it had been threadbare, shabby and full of holes.

"And you'll be taking me to Casimir," added Lewis persuasively. "It's not as if I'm going anywhere on my own. And Casimir might call you, you know, and you'd never get out of here with the window shut!"

The carpet thought about it and then lifted gently into the air. Lewis pulled a blanket off the bed and folding it up, spread it over the carpet, for the snow still lay deep over Edinburgh. He ran to the window and opened it wide so that he and the carpet could get through and a few minutes later they were soaring over the city towards Arthur's Seat.

So he had been right, he thought, as the hill loomed nearer. Casimir *had* gone to the friends he had told him about; the MacArthurs, the magic people that lived inside Arthur's Seat. The air was frosty and cold and Arthur's Seat was deep in snow as the carpet sailed towards it and he wondered apprehensively how on earth he was going to get in. He needn't have worried, however, as the carpet had been there many times before. The tunnel entrance was cunningly hidden but it knew its way and slid deftly with the ease of long practice, into the hill.

Lewis switched on his torch as the carpet sailed downwards through the inky blackness of a tunnel that seemed to go on for ever. Would it never end, he wondered. And just when he thought it never would, the carpet sailed into a huge cavern, brightly lit by blazing torches in iron sconces that were fastened to the walls.

As the carpet sailed into the cavern, Lewis almost fell off in fright, for the first thing he saw was a huge dragon, its scales glittering red in the light of the torches. Even as he gaped at it in wonder, it sent a stream of bright, sparkling fire across the cavern in a blaze of heat. Casimir had never mentioned a dragon and Lewis, keeping his balance only by a miracle, looked at it in awe as his carpet circled round and took him to a raised dais where several people were seated round a high throne. Thank goodness! Relief flooded through him. One of them was Casimir! His carpet drew closer and although he'd half guessed what to expect, his jaw nevertheless dropped at the sight of Sir James!

Everyone stared at him in amazement and, as he got off the carpet, he felt suddenly lonely and awkward. Casimir had told him about the MacArthur, however, and he'd no hesitation in picking out the strange, regal little figure perched on his throne. He bowed to him and waited.

"Welcome to the hill, Lewis," the MacArthur said. "Or should I call you 'The Shadow?'"

"I *was* the Shadow," Lewis admitted. "With Ca ... Prince Casimir, that is."

Casimir grinned at him sourly. "Lewis was learning!"

"So this is Lewis?" the Sultan said.

Lewis looked up as he recognized both the face and the voice. It was the Sultan of the pantomime!

"Make your bow," the MacArthur said, "to His Majesty, Sulaiman the Red, Sultan of Turkey!"

So involved had Lewis become in the affairs of the world of magic that this actually came as no surprise at all and he bowed low as he had seen Casimir do on stage. Even as he straightened, a huge eagle spread its wings. Amgarad, he thought, and its master, Lord Rothlan. The goblin at Ardray had talked about them.

Then there was Casimir! "I had to come, Prince Casimir!" he said, going up to him and grasping both his hands, "I wanted to help you and I … well, I thought you might need your carpet."

At a nod from the MacArthur, Sir James got to his feet and, smiling at Lewis reassuringly, introduced him to the others: Lord Alasdair Rothlan, Lady Ellan and several of the MacArthurs who sat on cushions by the chairs. Archie, Hamish and Jaikie got to their feet and, eyeing him with interest, shook his hand. Sir James then took him towards another man in Highland dress who rose to his feet as they approached. "And this," he said, "is Neil and Clara's father, John MacLean, and their mother, Janet."

The black crow perched on John MacLean's shoulder, fluttered its wings.

"And Kitor," Janet MacLean smiled, her hand reaching up to stroke the crow's black feathers, "Clara's crow!"

"And that," Archie said, indicating the dragon, "is Arthur, our dragon." At the mention of its name, the dragon let loose another burst of flames and turned its great head towards them. Archie grinned. "I'll take you over to meet him properly afterwards. He's not in a very good mood just now.

A bit upset that Neil and Clara have been kidnapped, you know."

Sir James interrupted. "You were in the audience this evening, Lewis, and you saw what happened. We've just been wondering how we can get Neil and Clara back from Prince Kalman."

"Why does Prince Kalman hate them so much?" Lewis asked.

"He hates Clara more than he hates Neil," the Sultan said, taking charge of the conversation. "It was Clara who spoke the magic words that broke the spell round the crown. They were my words and I was able to take my crown back from him when she said them."

"Where have they gone? Do you know?" Lewis asked, looking around.

"That's what is troubling us," the Sultan admitted. "Prince Kalman has used a hex to hide them from the world of magic. We can find no trace of them in our crystals. No trace at all."

28. Kalman's Revenge

Neil and Clara shivered violently as they recovered from their surprise at Kalman's hex and opened their eyes. The warmth of the blazing spotlights in the theatre had vanished the minute the prince had grasped their arms and now they found themselves in freezing blackness.

Neil sensed that the prince was still with them. "Where are we?" he asked, his voice echoing strangely.

"You are where no one will ever find you," Kalman said, his voice casual and cruel.

Clara put out her hand and drew it back swiftly as she touched a rocky wall that wasn't only icy cold but ran with moisture. Were they in a cave, perhaps?

At that moment, Kalman hexed up a couple of burning torches and stuck them into cracks in the wall. They looked round in wonder at their prison as the flaring flames flickered and glowed. It was, as they had suspected, a cave; a big cave with a towering ceiling that disappeared into gloomy darkness over their heads. The openings of tunnels were outlined against the surrounding walls but on the far side, a stretch of water rippled and lapped against the cave's rocky shelf.

Even as they looked, the ripples surged and splashed as a huge head broke the surface and a monster reared its long neck up out of the waves.

Its face had a sly, predatory look and its scaly skin
was a blackish, grey colour mottled by patches of
livid green. Neil and Clara clutched at one another
in horror mixed with sudden understanding, and
knew instantly where they were. They had seen
this particular monster before and they hadn't
much liked her then, either.

"Nessie!" Clara mouthed at Neil.

"The Loch Ness Monster!" he whispered in
awe as more and more of the enormous beast
appeared, dwarfing the cave with her size. They
clung together, shivering with cold and fright. No
wonder Kalman was so sure they'd never be found!
These must be Nessie's caves, hundreds of feet
under the mountains!

The monster dragged her great bulk out of the
water, sending waves surging in powerful ripples
across the floor until she finally managed to heave
herself onto the rocky platform.

"Prince Kalman!" she sounded surprised and more
than a little suspicious. "What brings you here?"

"Am I not welcome, then?" the prince said with
a low bow. "Grechan always speaks well of you and
I have come to ask you a favour, milady."

The monster didn't exactly preen herself but,
Neil thought shrewdly, the prince certainly knew
how to handle her.

"A favour, is it? Well, what do you wish of me,
Kalman?" Then she saw Neil and Clara. "Who are
those children?" she demanded.

Neil and Clara moved forward. "Bow!" Neil
muttered, as he bent at the waist. "Go on, Clara,
as low as you can!"

Kalman looked at them sourly. "Two children that I want to hide from the eyes of Sulaiman the Red."

"The Sultan?" Nessie said, impressed. She eyed them interestedly. "But they're surely too young to pose a threat to you?"

"They've meddled in my plans and need punishing," he said. "I'd be glad if you'd keep them here until Grechan arrives. Then, *he* can take charge of them. They'll be no bother. Feed them sparingly and they'll behave!"

Neil's heart sank at his words. This didn't sound too good!

Nessie moved towards them and so awed were they at her towering bulk that they failed to notice the arrival of several other strange creatures that had bobbed to the surface of the water in her wake. The mention of Grechan should have warned them that they'd be around and as the grey, shiny little creatures hoisted themselves effortlessly into the cave, Neil nudged Clara. Their noses wrinkled at the musty smell that emanated from them. Both knew immediately what they were — water goblins!

Attracted by the shining colours of their Ali Baba costumes that glowed brightly in the light of the torches, the water goblins flapped forward on webbed feet, their red eyes gleaming in their dome-like heads. They crowded round, fascinated by the glittering silk of their costumes and as their long fingers stretched out curiously, Neil and Clara shrank away from them. Nessie, however, saw what was happening and as her tail lashed threateningly, the goblins immediately backed off, looking resentful.

Nessie stared at Neil and Clara thoughtfully. "Do you know, Prince Kalman," she said, her expression suddenly turning very unpleasant indeed, "I think I recognise these children." Her huge head on its long neck bent over Neil. "You know the MacArthurs, don't you?" she hissed. "Weren't you both with Lady Ellan when she brought my Arthur to Loch Ness?"

They cowered back, nodding, too scared to speak.

"And you know that my Arthur came here and then left without even saying goodbye to me and quite broke my heart," she said, her voice rising. "I'll never forgive him, never!" Her tail lashed the floor of the cave angrily, sweeping several unwary goblins into the water. "And, let me tell you," her voice lowered threateningly, "that if you're his friends, I've a good mind to keep you here for ever and ever!"

She was so furious that, had she been a dragon, she'd probably have burnt them to a cinder there and then. As it was, she looked so fearsome that Neil and Clara took to their heels and ran, helter-skelter, into the first tunnel they came to.

Nessie frowned as Prince Kalman made no attempt to stop them.

Now Nessie had her moods and although she was quick to lose her temper she was equally quick in making up — but Neil and Clara, she suddenly realized, weren't to know this and now that they'd run off into the tunnels, she looked after them apprehensively, wishing that she hadn't been quite so dramatic.

"Leave them," Kalman shrugged, his voice casual. "With any luck they'll get lost in the tunnels and we'll never hear of them again." He bowed mockingly to Nessie. "If they *do* turn up, you can give them to Grechan. If they don't ... well, give him my regards, anyway. Tell him I'll be back soon!"

And with that, Kalman muttered a hex and promptly disappeared.

29. Kabad to the Rescue

"Stop, Clara," Neil gasped, his lungs bursting. "Stop! We've run far enough and nobody's chasing us."

Clara leant against the wall of the tunnel, clutching her side. She had a stitch and her breath was coming in great gasps. Never in her life had she felt so scared.

"Where are you, Neil?" she panted. "I can't see you. It's so dark and ..." she shivered, "I'm freezing cold."

Neil walked towards the sound of her voice. "I can't help it," she said, her teeth chattering. "It's just fright that's making me all shivery."

What they needed, Neil thought, was some warmer clothes for the thin, silky stuff of their pantomime costume was no protection whatsoever against the freezing draught that edged sharply along the tunnel.

"I think we should go back," Neil said, "while we remember the way."

"No! How can you even think about it? Nessie's horrible!!"

"She can't be all that bad if Arthur likes her. And he does, you know."

"Well ..." she sounded doubtful.

"We'll freeze if we don't keep moving," Neil insisted, "and if we go any further, we might get lost." So, arms outstretched, they made their way back the way they had come. At least they thought they did. It was only much later when they'd stumbled along for a good half hour that Neil called a halt. "We must have missed a turning," he admitted, anxiously. "We didn't run from Nessie for more than a few minutes. We're lost, Clara!"

"Shhhh!" Clara grabbed Neil's arm. "I can hear something! Listen …"

It was a strange flapping noise and it was coming closer. Clara stuffed her knuckles in her mouth to stop herself from screaming.

"Are you there?" a voice whispered. They heard it in their heads, in much the same way as they heard Kitor and Amgarad.

Neil relaxed thankfully for it didn't sound like a terribly fierce voice. "Yes, we're here," he answered, guessing that the flapping noise was the sound of webbed feet. "Who are you? Are you a water goblin?"

"Yes, my name is Kabad. I … I thought you might be lost."

"We are," Neil answered. "Thank goodness you came to look for us! Was it Nessie that sent you? Or the prince?"

"No, I came on my own. I was Arthur's friend when he was here, you see. I liked him and he told me lots of stories about the MacArthurs and Archie and Arthur's Seat."

Knowing that Arthur would never have chatted about Archie and the MacArthurs to anyone he didn't like, reassured Clara. "I think he really wants to help us, Neil," she whispered.

Neil nodded and although Clara couldn't see him, she sensed that he agreed with her. "Kabad, we want to speak to Nessie about Arthur but she was so angry with us that we're a bit afraid."

Kabad sounded doubtful. "She'll probably be all right when she calms down."

"You see, Nessie doesn't really understand why Arthur left. He was homesick for the hill, worried about his treasure and … oh, lots of other things. I'm sure he wants to come back and see her but I think he's afraid she might be angry. Could you tell her that?"

There was a silence. "Nessie sometimes eats goblins when she is hungry, or if they make her angry," Kabad said fearfully.

"Kabad," Clara said, remembering the goblins' fascination for their clothes, "if you do what Neil asks then I'll … I'll give you my shiny clothes."

Kabad hissed as he thought of the clothes. Never, in his whole life, had he seen such wonderful things and his heart swelled at the thought of owning them. Of course, he told himself, he would never be able to wear them except in secret, for the other goblins would be jealous and take them from him but … but perhaps he could hide them somewhere safe and take them out to look at from time to time …

Clara felt sorry for the little creature, understanding how much he was tempted. She remembered how she'd felt when she'd first tried on the costume in the dressing room in the Assembly Hall; how excited she'd been when the silk glinted and glittered in the lights.

"I'll do it," Kabad said.

"We'll follow you back through the tunnels, then," Neil said in relief. "We're totally lost!"

Kabad's webbed fingers gripped Neil's hand and Clara held onto the back of his tunic as they made their way back through the darkness of the tunnels to the main cavern where the torches still burned.

"You'd better stay here just now," Kabad said, his voice shaky as he steeled himself to talk to the Great Lady.

Peering out from the entrance to the tunnel, they watched as Kabad make his way through a scattered crowd of water goblins towards Nessie. He bowed low to her and Clara crossed her fingers as the surprised goblins crowded round to hear what was going on. Kabad spoke to Nessie at length but from what they could see, she didn't seem terribly impressed.

"I hope he hasn't blown it," Neil groaned.

At that moment, one of the water goblins in the crowd made what was to prove an unfortunate remark about Arthur.

In an instant, Nessie's expression changed to one of utter fury, and the cackle of evil laughter that had echoed round the cave, quickly died away as the wary goblins realized that they'd overstepped the mark by a couple of miles. Roaring with rage, her tail lashing furiously, she cleared the cave of goblins in seconds. Only Kabad stood his ground and once she had calmed down, Nessie listened to him more carefully.

Minutes later he ran up, smiling his funny, goblin

smile. "It's all right," he assured them. "Nessie says she didn't mean to frighten you."

Neil took a deep breath. "I think it's okay, Clara," he said. "Anyhow, we'll just have to chance it."

"Well," Nessie said, looking at them grimly as they came towards her. "I don't know what you've been up to but you seem to have made a bad enemy of the prince."

Neil and Clara nodded.

"It's not my business," she continued. "It's for you to sort things out with Kalman. But what's this that Kabad's been telling me about Arthur?"

"You really mustn't be angry with Arthur," said Neil, "I'm sure he likes you, but after the way he left, I think he's maybe afraid to come back to see you."

"He was worried at leaving his treasure," interrupted Clara. "While he was here the last time, someone stole his firestones and Lord Rothlan and his army got into the hill ... into Arthur's Seat."

"Hmmm!" Nessie said thoughtfully. "Yes, I heard about that."

"And he was homesick, too. He's lived with the MacArthurs for hundreds of years, you know, and ... well, he missed them!"

"But he had *me!*" snorted Nessie, rearing majestically and looking thoroughly put out. "Wasn't that enough?"

"Yes, of course," Clara said hurriedly, "but you're not always here, are you?" she pointed out. "You spend a lot of time out in the loch finding fish to eat."

"The thing is," Neil said, "that Arthur doesn't like fish much and ..."

"And some of your water goblins weren't very nice to him ..." Clara added, her fingers crossed behind her back.

"All sorts of things worried him, milady, especially his treasure but he didn't want to mention it to you."

"He should have done!" Nessie said, sitting up straight.

"He's really very fond of you," Neil said.

"The dear creature!" Nessie murmured, "is he really?"

"Yes, of course he is," smiled Clara. "I'm sure he'd like to visit you again but ..."

"But what?" demanded Nessie.

"If you could give him a sign, he'd come at once! To visit you, you know ... and it would be nice for us to see him again, too. Why, we could keep one another company while you were out fishing."

"But Grechan will be here soon to take you to his caves," Nessie said, "and Prince Kalman wants to hide you from the Sultan!"

"But not from the MacArthurs, milady," Neil said. "The decision is up to you, though. Wouldn't you like to see Arthur again and let him explain things for himself?"

Now Nessie was genuinely fond of Arthur and the thought of seeing him again set her heart beating fast. "But how can I get in touch with him?" she asked despairingly. "How can I tell him that I want to see him again?"

Neil unwound the length of striped silk that served as his turban. "If you swim round Loch Ness waving this," he said, "someone would be sure to see it. You're really famous in Scotland, you know. The television cameras would be there, everyone would be watching you. You'd be on TV!"

Nessie had been bored for too long to turn down such an inviting suggestion. She'd no idea what *teevee* was, but it was obviously something wonderful. "I'll do it!" she said decisively. "Give me the flag!"

"It's no good going just now, Nessie," Clara said. "It's night time and it'll still be dark outside."

"Yes," agreed Neil. "No one will be able to see you until tomorrow morning when the sun comes up."

"Oh, that's not a problem," Nessie said, casually. "I can make today into tomorrow quite easily."

Clara felt a spinning sensation and looked at Neil who shook his head dizzily.

"There," Nessie said comfortably, "that's that done. Now, Neil, give me the flag and I'll be off! I can't *wait* to see my Arthur again!"

Neil handed her the strip of purple and gold silk and they watched in relief as without any further ado, she grasped it in her mouth, slid off the rocky shelf and disappeared below the waves.

30. Nessie flies the Flag

In the huge cavern under Arthur's Seat, time passed slowly and still there was no news of Neil and Clara.

"Every bird and beast in Scotland is on the lookout for them," the MacArthur assured the Ranger. "The stags on the mountains, the grouse on the moors and the sea-birds round the coast. They're all on the alert but nothing's turned up so far."

"I know you're doing everything you can," the Ranger said, "it's just that Janet's making herself ill. She didn't sleep at all last night!"

"We'll find them, don't worry! Even Kitor and Amgarad are out searching for them. They've gone over to the west coast and are checking the mountains round Ardray. It's only a matter of time before they're found, believe me."

Although his voice was calm, the MacArthur was nevertheless seriously worried and so, too, was the Sultan, who felt personally responsible for the danger they were in. They were all doing their bit, however. Jaikie, Hamish and Archie were taking it in turns to monitor the crystal round the clock and Casimir and the Sultan had gone to Morven with Lord Rothlan to visit the Lords of the North, hoping that with their help the children would soon be found. He sighed. It was difficult to know what else could be done!

Hope suddenly sprang in his heart, however, as he noticed two of the magic carpets unfurling themselves and setting off across the cavern.

"Whose are they?" the Ranger asked, turning his head to watch them leave.

"One is Sir James's," answered the MacArthur, "and I think the other is the one we gave to Lewis."

"Let's hope they have some news at last!" the Ranger said, his voice lightening.

Sir James and Lewis arrived on their magic carpets at much the same time. Both had been watching lunchtime television and had seen the same thing. So excited were they that they almost fell off their carpets as they approached the MacArthur and could barely speak so full were they of their news.

"The Loch Ness Monster!" Lewis said excitedly.

"She's on television!" added Sir James.

"What?" Arthur, the great dragon, sat up straight as the MacArthur leapt to his feet, relief sweeping through him.

"She's on television," Sir James repeated. "All the channels are full of it!"

"This morning," Lewis said, "people driving along the side of the road saw her and phoned Sky News. They're getting loads of pictures of her! And she *wants* them to see her! She's cruising up and down Loch Ness like a ... like a movie star!"

Sir James strode over to the Ranger. "That's not the most important thing, though," he said gripping him by the shoulders. "She's got something in her mouth ... "

"Purple and gold," nodded Lewis, his eyes shining.

"It's part of Neil and Clara's costume, John. She's showing us where they are!"

"Thank goodness!" the Ranger said shakily. "I ... I must go and tell Janet!"

"Wait a minute, Ranger," Hamish said, adjusting the crystal. "Don't go yet. I can find her in a minute. There ... there she is! Look!"

Even Arthur lumbered over, his head rearing above them as they crowded round the crystal. Sure enough, there was Nessie! Urquhart Castle loomed in the background as she sailed up and down Loch Ness in all her majesty, carrying a floaty piece of silk in her mouth. Everyone recognized it. Striped in purple and gold, it was part of one of the pantomime costumes.

Jaikie then turned the eye of the crystal towards the shore. The mountains, covered in snow, gleamed in the pale rays of a winter sun and, as he focused on the road, they could see that cars were parked all along the edge of the loch. People swarmed along the shoreline and, not only that, several boats had taken to the water and were venturing up to her.

Lady Ellan, who had seen the carpets streaking through the cavern, now joined them. "Nessie!" she said with a snap in her voice, "and her fine friend, Grechan, I've no doubt!" She looked at her father angrily. "We should have guessed, father! They were always Kalman's friends!"

"Let Nessie know we are watching her," the MacArthur said. "Some of these boats are getting

a bit too close for my liking and she only needs to
flap her tail to sink half of them!"

Although it couldn't be seen in daylight, Nessie
felt the warmth of the ray of light from the crystal
that held her in its beam and knew immediately
that she had been seen by the world of magic.
Hoping fervently that it was the MacArthurs who
had homed in on her, she tossed her head once more
so that the stream of purple and gold silk flew like
a flag in the wind and then, in an almighty swirl
of water that tossed the boats in a violent surge,
she dived below the cold, grey waters of Loch Ness
and disappeared.

31. Showdown

The MacArthur looked round the gathering thoughtfully and addressed the Sultan. "I've had a talk with Arthur, your majesty. He says, quite definitely, that he has to be the one to rescue Neil and Clara. He ... er, says that his Nessie sometimes gets into a funny temper but he thinks he can handle her."

The Sultan cleared his throat. "Does anyone have any other ideas?" he asked, looking round enquiringly. Amgarad spread his great wings and looked at Kitor. Both birds knew that they could do nothing while Neil and Clara were under Loch Ness.

"I think I should go," Casimir stood up and bowed to the Sultan and the MacArthur. "Prince Kalman is my son and I must try to make him see reason!"

Lewis dropped his eyes. From what he'd seen of Kalman, he didn't think old Casimir had much of a chance. No one spoke but their silence was eloquent. Casimir flushed and Lewis sprang to his feet.

"I'll go with Casimir," he said, "it's his right to see his son even if he might not be able to persuade him. I can be the Shadow again, Casimir," he said, going up and looking into his eyes. "Come on, we make a great team! Remember the Forth Bridge? What a day that was!"

Casimir was touched and smiled wryly. "I couldn't have chosen a better person to rescue me from the well at Al Antara, Lewis," he said abruptly. "Thank you, but I don't want you to be put at risk. The Sultan will tell you that the situation is dangerous."

The Sultan, his brown eyes watchful, leant forward in his chair. "I think Arthur is right," he announced. "He should go to see Nessie first and then you, Casimir, should talk with your son. As Lewis says," he said, smiling approvingly at Lewis, "you are his father and it is your right."

Sir James rubbed his chin. "Loch Ness is heaving with TV crews and reporters," he pointed out. "Arthur will be seen."

The Sultan smiled. "We'll get the storm carriers to take care of them," he said, "and with any luck, it won't be long before you have your children back, Ranger!"

The storm swept in from the north on a roaring, tearing wind. The skies above Loch Ness darkened swiftly from a steely grey to a brownish purple and, given the sudden, total lack of visibility, the TV crews grimaced, packed up their cameras, and, lashed by the storm, headed for nearby Drumnadrochit while the many small boats on the lookout for Nessie, hurriedly made for safety as the waters of the loch rose in black, threatening waves around them.

Arthur came in on the skirts of a black cloud that quite successfully hid him from view and, taking his bearings from the ruins of Urquhart

Castle, swooped swiftly down into the icy waters of Loch Ness. Deeper and deeper he dived until he saw the grim, dark opening of Nessie's caves loom black before him. After that it was easy and swimming strongly he negotiated the series of passages that ran steadily upwards until he finally surfaced in Nessie's lair.

The water goblins that were there to see his arrival almost had heart failure. Another monster! They streaked into the tunnels and passages for safety and then crowded the entrances to peek out and see what this fearsome new creature was like. Hearing the shrieks and screams that accompanied Arthur's arrival, Neil and Clara ran to see what was happening, pushing their way through a mass of excited, chattering goblins who by then had recognized Arthur as a friend.

"Thank goodness," Neil said, relief ringing in his voice, "Arthur's arrived!"

"It's all right, Kabad," Clara said reassuringly to the little goblin who clung to her hand, "it's Arthur. He's come to see Nessie! Didn't we tell you he would?"

Watching from the side of the cave, Neil and Clara saw Nessie and Arthur meet. Arthur flapped his wings and seemed truly delighted to see her again while Nessie, who had forgotten her anger, waltzed about delightedly. The goblins, however, weren't quite so happy. Accustomed as they were to keeping well out of the way of Nessie's massive bulk, they were quite frankly finding two monsters a bit of a nightmare to cope with. In fact, they had to be pretty nippy on their feet to avoid being trampled on.

"Neil and Clara said you would come, Arthur!" Nessie said happily. "And here you are!"

The celebrations came to an abrupt halt, however, when a sudden crack and a puff of smoke announced the arrival of Prince Kalman. One look at the prince was enough. He was in a towering rage.

"You fool!" he snapped at Nessie, "you complete and utter fool! Don't you realize that you've given the game away completely?"

"I hope I can invite my friends to visit when I wish," Nessie said sulkily. "I happen to live here, you know." Then she added in a stronger voice. "These are *my* caves, after all! Why shouldn't I invite Arthur to visit me when I please?"

"That's why you were out there then, was it?" the prince ground out, disbelief colouring his voice. "Attracting the world! Behaving like a lunatic! Waving a flag! What on earth's got into you?"

"How dare you speak to my Nessie like that, Prince Kalman," Arthur said hotly.

Nessie batted her long eyelashes at Arthur and Kalman, to give him his due, winced noticeably at this display of affection. It was really too, too much. Monsters were bad enough at the best of times but there obviously wasn't a lot one could do with this pair of love-sick loonies! Added to which, he thought warily, one of them was a dragon and although he would have like to have said a great deal more, caution prevailed. He took a deep breath and curbed his tongue.

"Where are Neil and Clara?" he snapped.

As everyone turned to look at them, a horrible silence fell.

"It was a plot, wasn't it," he grated, looking furiously at Arthur, "it was all a plot to get the children back!"

It was when Arthur blew a gentle stream of fire as a warning that the prince realized he had been defeated; for over the years he had seen smaller dragons than Arthur in action and had no wish to end up as a burnt-out cinder!

Even as he swallowed this bitter pill, however, there was another crack and a puff of smoke. The water goblins who hadn't had this much excitement in years, screamed and clutched at one another in alarm. Neil and Clara scanned the cave; they knew that another magician must have arrived, but who was it? Prince Kalman, too, swung round, a hex at the ready, half expecting it to be the Sultan, himself.

"It's Prince Casimir," Neil said, gripping Clara's arm.

"Father," Kalman gasped.

"Kalman," Prince Casimir's voice filled with emotion as he gazed on his son. "Kalman, we must talk."

"Speak! I am listening," Kalman threw up a hand, his voice hard and unfriendly.

"The Sultan ..."

"Don't talk to me about the Sultan. *You* might be his vassal but I'll never bend my knee to him! Never!"

"Kalman! You are my son! The past is over. Please, I beg you ... forget your enmity towards the Sultan." Casimir held out his arms in silent appeal but the prince stood rigid and unbending, his face a cold mask.

"*Your* enmity might have changed," Kalman said coldly, "but mine has not. Don't forget that *I* found the crown! It was mine! I had such power … and he took it from me! I will never forgive him and nor should you!"

Hopelessly, his father dropped his arms by his side, looking devastated.

Neil looked at Kalman with complete contempt, knowing full well that the crown had belonged to the Sultan and that he had no claim to it.

Kalman must have read his thoughts for his eyes shone with such fury that Neil stepped back startled and Casimir flung out an arm to protect him.

Seeing Kalman's rage, Arthur thought it time to intervene. Indeed, the blazing stream of fire he sent curling across the floor of the cave stopped the prince in his tracks quite successfully, and did much to remind him of the delicacy of his situation.

Taking a deep breath, he looked round grimly as he realized that given the circumstances, there wasn't a lot he could do. His face, however, betrayed no emotion and, deciding then and there to cut his losses, he bowed low to his father and then, rather mockingly to Arthur and Nessie. No one moved to stop him as he murmured the words of a hex and in an instant, disappeared.

There was an awful silence that nobody dared break. Casimir put his hands over his face and stood perfectly still, looking totally bereft.

"We're very sorry, Prince Casimir," Neil said quietly.

"Really sorry," added Clara.

Casimir dropped his hands and looked at them both steadily. He sighed and gave a somewhat shaky smile. "Come," he said as calmly as he was able, "I can do no more here. I must take you back to the hill. Your parents are anxious to see you."

Clara felt Kabad tug desperately at her tunic and looked down at him. Her face softened. She knew that she couldn't leave him behind. The other water goblins had turned out to be little more than particularly horrible bullies. Really nasty creeps, she thought. They'd been jealous of him when they'd found out what he'd done and from then on had made his life miserable, sneaking up on him and pinching him when they thought she wasn't looking. Indeed, they'd been so horrible to him that in the end he hadn't dared leave her. As she prised his frantic fingers from edge of her tunic, his face crumpled in an agony of fear and apprehension. "Don't leave me here," he pleaded desperately. "Please, Clara!"

"Don't worry, I'm not going to leave you, Kabad," she said reassuringly. "Neil and I would like you to come home with us, wouldn't we, Neil?" she said.

"Yes, of course,' he said, smiling. "There's a nice loch quite near our house. You'll like it there." There were hisses of anger and envy from the other water goblins but Neil ignored them and looked hopefully at Nessie. It was up to her. What if she wouldn't let them take Kabad?

"Is that all right, Nessie?" Clara queried. "Can we take Kabad with us?"

Nessie, totally taken up with Arthur, nodded quite happily. What was one water goblin, after all? As far as she was concerned, they could take a couple of dozen. One would certainly never be missed.

Neil met Casimir's eyes and grinned. "Is that all right with you, Prince Casimir?" he asked.

Despite himself, Casimir smiled as he saw the ridiculous grin that had spread over the little water goblin's face.

"Quite all right," he said.

Clara turned to Nessie and Arthur. "Goodbye," she waved, "and thank you both!"

"Bye, Arthur!" Neil said. "Bye, Nessie! Take care!"

Casimir then held his hands over them, murmured the words of a spell and a startled Arthur and Nessie suddenly found that, in the twinkling of an eye, all their magic visitors had left.

32. Christmas Party

A few days after Prince Casimir brought Neil and Clara safely back from Loch Ness, the MacArthur decided to throw a party; a Christmas party. They were all there, except Arthur, who had decided to stay for a while with his Nessie in Loch Ness.

Neil and Clara weren't sure if the MacArthur hadn't had a hand in arranging the weather to suit the occasion, for it was a positively magical scene. Snow was falling gently and as the MacLeans flew towards the hill on their magic carpets, Edinburgh stretched beneath them like a huge Christmas card. Once inside, they gasped in wonder for the tunnels were lit by hundreds of fairy lights and the great cavern, strung as it was from wall to wall with Christmas decorations, lanterns and dozens of brightly lit Christmas trees, was a sparkling fairyland of light and colour.

"It looks wonderful," Clara smiled, hugging Lady Ellan.

"I'm glad you like it," she smiled, as Amgarad swooped down to land on Clara's shoulder. "We've been busy as you can see! Actually, Archie, Hamish and Jaikie did most of it!"

Jaikie, perched at the top of a ladder, waved down to them as he fixed a star at the top of the tall Christmas tree that stood beside the MacArthur's throne.

Lewis laughed and waved back. "I can't quite

believe it all, Neil," he said, marvelling at the sight. "It's fab, isn't it?"

Kabad came shyly over wearing his striped pantomime clothes. Mrs MacLean had shortened them for him and they sparkled in the light of the torches. He had never seen a Christmas tree before and gazed up at it in wonder. What with the tree, the decorations and his fabulous new clothes, he was the happiest water goblin in the world.

"Is the Sultan able to come?" Sir James asked as he and the Chief Constable added some brightly wrapped packages to the pile of Christmas gifts under the huge tree.

"Yes," Lord Rothlan answered, "he's at Ardray at the moment with Prince Casimir. Sorting out last minute business and the like."

Lewis heard him. "He's gone to Ardray?" he said in astonishment. "But Ardray was destroyed. All that was left was a sort of pillar of energy!"

"The Sultan has already restored Ardray," Lady Ellan said with a smile, "according to Alasdair, the estate is completely different now."

"You went there, Lord Rothlan?" Neil asked, his eyes round.

Alasdair Rothlan nodded. "You wouldn't recognize it, Neil. The Sultan blotted out the magic forest and the Black Tower and has replaced them with a beautiful castle that is set closer to the sea. Casimir is delighted with it and I think he plans to invite us there once he's got it all fixed up."

"Prince Casimir's all right, is he?" Lewis asked anxiously.

"Here he is now," Lord Rothlan said as the

Sultan and Prince Casimir stepped through the gilded frame of the magic mirror. "You can ask him yourself!"

Everyone bowed as the Sultan appeared but Lewis ran straight to Casimir and hugged him. "I'm so glad to see you!" he said. "You look really well!" Indeed, they all looked at Casimir in astonishment. The Sultan's generosity had been such that there was no room for discontent and his face, now calm and untroubled, was kindly and pleasant. His eyes twinkled as he looked at Lewis.

"You haven't changed a bit, Lewis," he said, with a sigh. "Where's your bow to the Sultan!"

Lewis reddened and bowed hastily to the Sultan.

"Don't worry, Lewis," the Sultan smiled, "we all understand your concern for Prince Casimir."

The ice was broken and it was only after they had finished eating an absolutely massive Christmas dinner of turkey and Christmas pudding that they all sat, chatting idly together round the table.

Prince Casimir looked across at Sir James and asked about the pantomime. "Is *Ali Baba* still running, Sir James?" he queried.

"Oh yes," Sir James nodded. "It doesn't finish until the middle of January."

"And are Neil and Clara still taking part?" asked the Chief Constable, looking across the table in surprise. "Sorry, I've been busy. I meant to ask earlier."

Neil and Clara both nodded. "Matt Lafferty gave us a really funny look when we turned up again, though," Clara grinned.

"Gob-smacked is the word he'd have used!" Neil said.

"And he looked absolutely floored," Clara added, "when I had to have a new costume made!"

"And I needed a new turban! I gave mine to Nessie to use as a flag and I'm sure he recognized it from the TV footage," Neil said with a grin. "He knows that something odd was going on the night we disappeared and I think he's guessed that magic was involved!"

"An intelligent man," nodded the Sultan, his eyes twinkling.

"He doesn't miss much," Sir James agreed, "but, you know, even *he* will be hard put to make up a story that'll link you to the Loch Ness monster!"

There was a murmur of laughter.

"I do miss Arthur," Clara said sadly. "Don't you, Archie? I know he's happy with Nessie but there's not a lot to do at the bottom of Loch Ness."

"He'll stay a few months and then come back," Archie sighed. "I wish he hadn't missed our Christmas party, though."

"What I'd really like to know is what happened to the bank robbers?" Clara asked. "Did you catch them, Sir Archie?"

"We only caught two of them," Sir Archie replied, "Murdo and Tammy Souter. Wullie managed to slip through the net."

At Clara's questioning stare, the MacArthur chipped in. "You *did* hear what happened to Wullie, didn't you?"

Lady Ellan burst out laughing at the mention of his name. "He was fantastic," she said. "The ghosts of the plague victims didn't stand a chance against Wullie! Not a chance!"

At that, both Neil and Clara sat up straight and looked at one another in horror. "You mean the ghosts of the plague got out?" Neil gasped.

"Yes," she said, startled. "I'm sorry! I forgot you didn't know! Yes, when the crooks blew up the vault, the explosion knocked down the walls of their cellars. Mary King's ghosts got all the policemen out safely, thank goodness, but they somehow managed to miss Wullie."

"You don't mean ..." Neil looked stricken, "you don't mean ...?"

"Nothing happened to Wullie," Lady Ellan grinned despite herself. "The plague ghosts went for him, of course, but would you believe it, he killed them off! All by himself!"

"Wullie?" Clara said. "I thought he was a bit ... well, he wasn't sharp like Murdo."

"Make no mistake," laughed Lady Ellan. "Wullie was marvellous!"

"It was his cigarettes that finished them off," nodded the MacArthur with a grin. "He absolutely reeked of tobacco smoke and they couldn't take it!"

"Especially when he flapped his overcoat at them," added Jaikie. "That's what *really* did for them! They just fizzled up and died!"

"I still can't believe it!" Sir Archie said. "To tell you the truth, I don't know what we'd have done if it hadn't been for Wullie! The very thought of the Plague People getting out into the streets still gives me nightmares."

"Have all the ghosts gone back to Mary King's Close now?" asked the Ranger.

It was the MacArthur who answered. "Well, we had a bit of trouble about that," he said, leaning back in his chair. "The Plague People put them in a blind panic, as you can imagine. Once they'd seen your policemen safe in the Assembly Hall, Sir Archie, I'm afraid they just lost their heads. Some of them went up to the castle but most of them moved down to Holyrood Palace and well ... you know how it is, they got accustomed to living in style and didn't fancy moving back to the High Street."

Jaikie grinned. "And you can just imagine what happened when they first arrived at the palace!" he grinned. "Believe me, it was absolutely manic! They scared the living daylights out of the tourists for a start and, in the end, the staff had to close the palace altogether!"

"Rizzio," Lady Ellan said seriously, "was not amused."

"You can't blame him," the MacArthur said, reasonably. "After all, he's had the run of the palace for centuries!"

Jaikie grinned. "Apparently, he threw a thousand fits when they all poured in from the High Street. The very thought of them living in the *palace* ... well, I ask you! He's such a snob!"

Sir James and the Chief Constable looked at one another with lifted eyebrows. They both knew who David Rizzio was, of course. Italian by birth, he'd been secretary to Mary, Queen of Scots before her husband had murdered him!

Lewis smiled at the mention of his name and looked over at Casimir. He not only knew that Lord Darnley had murdered Rizzio but also knew the date — 1566.

"As Jaikie said, he was really furious," continued Ellan. "He called the Council of Elders to a meeting at the palace and demanded that all the ghosts be made invisible again and ordered to move back to their old quarters."

"Aye," said the MacArthur. "There was a real stramash about it but he won in the end."

"What, er … happened?" asked Sir James faintly.

"Well, it was Her Majesty!"

"The Queen?" said the Chief Constable, in tones of surprise.

"Aye," the MacArthur nodded, "as you know, she's always in residence in the summer. And, as Rizzio said, it just wasn't on. Her Majesty accepts *his* presence as a matter of course, you see, and he's very discreet. Just a dignified bow if he ever encounters her. But, as he said, she really shouldn't have to put up with half the High Street drifting through the walls of her apartments whenever they felt like it!"

"Not at all the done thing," said Sir James, keeping his face straight with an effort.

"Exactly!" said the MacArthur, heaving a sigh. "Anyway, it was all sorted out in the end. The Council of Elders made them all invisible again and they've already moved back up the High Street to Mary King's Close."

"And what about the bank?" Neil asked curiously. "I can't understand it. Dad told me it wasn't a branch any more but I see from the papers that quite a lot of money was taken."

Everyone looked at Sir Archie. "It *isn't* a branch anymore," he agreed, "it's a museum now, and normally, it wouldn't have held any money at all. But it turns out that the Bank of Scotland were in the process of refurbishing some of their branches and, well, I suppose they had to put the money somewhere. The empty vaults at the Mound were ideal for the purpose. It was just bad luck that Murdo, Wullie and Tammy decided to rob it when it was stuffed full of cash."

"And there's no doubt they took it," Sir James added, "for when we emptied the charity baskets in the foyer that were used for donations, we found bin-liners full of used notes at the bottom of most of them."

"Wow!" Clara's eyes grew large.

"Ali Baba and the Forty-Three Thieves," grinned Neil.

"I've good news for you, though," and here Sir James smiled happily. "The bank has been very generous and has made us a gift of the money we found, so we'll be able to send a much larger donation to Children's Aid than we thought! Much larger!" he added.

The Chief Constable, who knew exactly how much money the Bank of Scotland had quite happily shelled out, had his own ideas as to the origin of their sudden fit of reckless generosity and eyed the MacArthur with deep suspicion. The MacArthur, well-aware of what was going on in Sir Archie's mind, met his eyes blandly, however, and nodded with a smile at the excited murmur that greeted the news.

"Will the thieves be going to jail, then, Sir Archie?" Clara asked. "I didn't much like Murdo, but Wullie seemed a good sort."

The Chief Constable smiled wryly. "It's all been a bit difficult," he admitted, "and we've actually had to let them go." His eyes twinkled suddenly. "And to tell you the truth, I'm not sorry about it," he admitted, "not after what Wullie did! And, when all's said and done, I doubt if we'd have been able to bring any sort of case against them, anyway. The problem, really, was the ghosts — for we could hardly ask Mary King and her friends to testify, could we?"

Sir James smiled appreciatively at the thought of the ghosts in court. What a sensation that would have caused!

"I'm glad," Clara said happily. "I liked Wullie and he *did* save Edinburgh from the plague, didn't he!"

"Yes," Neil said, "but if they hadn't blown up the vault in the first place then the plague ghosts would never have got out! I reckon they've been lucky!"

The MacArthur and Lord Rothlan exchanged amused glances. They had both taken a liking to Wullie and had made quite sure that in facing up to the Plague People and saving the citizens of Edinburgh from the Black Death that he had been suitably and adequately rewarded.

33. Christmas Presents

"Talking of people being lucky," the MacArthur smiled at Neil and Clara, "I think there are two *very* lucky children here because all of the presents under the tree are our gifts to you for Christmas."

Neil and Clara looked delighted but eyed one another awkwardly, nevertheless. What about Lewis? Were there no presents for him?

"We'd like you to take them home and keep them until Christmas Day," Lady Ellan added, smiling understandingly at their discomfort, "so that you open them at the same time as Lewis."

Neil grinned. He might have known that they wouldn't forget Lewis.

"We've been doing a little scheming," Lord Rothlan admitted, placing an arm round Lewis's shoulders.

"You see, we can't actually give you presents to take home, Lewis," Lady Ellan said, "because your parents would wonder where they came from, but we *have* cast a spell so that you'll have quite a few more gifts than usual. I hope that's all right?"

"Thank you," Lewis said gratefully, feeling touched that they'd gone to so much trouble on his behalf.

The Sultan then stood up and beckoning Neil and Clara forward, held out two small packages wrapped in scarlet paper. "The MacArthur, Lord Rothlan and I,' he smiled, "have decided to give you each a very special, magic gift. Now that you've become so involved in our world we felt it suitable and sensible to give you some protection against its dangers."

Their excited smiles faded at the seriousness of his voice and their faces became attentive. "Thank you, your majesty," they said, looking somewhat doubtfully at the brightly-wrapped gifts.

"Open them, then," urged Lady Ellan with a smile. "They won't bite you, I promise!"

Hands trembling slightly, they tore off the wrapping paper to reveal small velvet boxes. They both knew what they were. Ring boxes. Clara flipped open the lid of her box and her face fell as she looked at the ring inside. She glanced across at Neil, who didn't look too impressed, either. They'd expected something bright, sparkling and exciting, not this plain band of rather dull silver. "Is it a magic ring?" she queried, trying to hide her disappointment as her eyes met those of the Sultan.

"I know they don't look very special," the Sultan apologised, his eyes twinkling as he glanced at Lord Rothlan and the MacArthur who were grinning broadly, "but they're made from a very special metal and I'm afraid there's not a lot we can do to improve their appearance."

"What do they do?" Clara asked, curiously.

"Well ... if you wear the ring on this finger," the Sultan said, indicating the third finger of Clara's right hand, "then nothing will happen, but if you slip it onto the ring finger of your *left* hand ... why don't you try it on and see for yourself."

"Okay," Clara smiled a trifle nervously as she lifted the ring carefully from its box, slipped it

onto the third finger of her left hand — and immediately disappeared.

"Clara!" her mother sprang to her feet. "Clara?
Where are you?"

"I'm still here, Mum," Clara's voice said, "Wow!
I ... I think I've just become invisible! This is fantastic! Neil! Lewis! Can you see me?" She reached
out and Lewis jumped as he felt her hand grab his
arm. It was the weirdest thing.

Neil's heart lifted excitedly as he looked around,
trying to see the slightest trace of Clara. "Come on,
Neil," her voice urged, "try yours on! It's amazing!
The magic rings make us invisible!"

She watched as Neil slipped his ring onto his
finger and promptly vanished as well.

"Crumbs," Neil said, walking round, "this is
great! It gives you a strange feeling, though, doesn't
it? Everybody looks ... not quite real, somehow."

She nodded and then remembered that he
couldn't see her. "Yes," she agreed, "it's ... well
... magicky. I can't see *you* at all now but I can
see mum, dad and everyone else through a sort of
gauze ... like a thin veil."

"Well, we can't see *you* through a veil," her father
said. "We can't see you at all — not even a shadow."

"There are one or two things to remember about
the rings," the Sultan said with a smile, "but we'll
tell you all about them later. Nothing at all to
worry about," he assured them, catching a glimpse
of Mrs MacLean's face.

"Could you take the ring off, now, Clara," her
mother said, trying not to sound too concerned. "I
want to see you appear again!"

"To see if it works both ways, you mean," said Neil.

"Don't worry about the children, Janet," the Sultan smiled, "they'll come to no harm."

Clara pulled off her ring and, transferring it to the third finger of her right hand, materialized the minute the switch was made. "Thank you, your majesty," she said, giving the Sultan a really delighted smile. "Honestly, I've never had a more wonderful present!"

"Absolutely brilliant," agreed Neil as he, too, pulled the ring from his finger. Never, in his wildest dreams had he expected anything like this. Magic rings! They were truly wonderful gifts but what meant more to him was the fact that the Sultan was trusting them with real magic.

"What if we lose the rings, though?" Clara looked at the Sultan worriedly. Her mother was always getting on to her about being untidy.

"You won't lose them," the Sultan shook his head. "Prince Casimir and I have seen to that."

Still thrilled at the thought of such a marvellous present, Neil spread his fingers and looked at it in wonder. He owned a magic ring! How cool was that!

Casimir now stood up and came forward. "I have a ring for you, too, Lewis," he said kindly, handing him a similar box to the ones the Sultan had given Neil and Clara, "a different kind of ring, but equally useful!"

Lewis tore the wrapping paper off and, as Neil and Clara peered over his shoulder, opened the ring box carefully.

"How lovely," Clara said. "It's beautiful, Lewis!"

"Thank you, Prince Casimir," Lewis said quietly, "thank you very much." He knew just by looking at it that this was a very special ring and one that he would never be parted from. It was much more ornate than the silvery bands that decorated Neil and Clara's fingers. It was a ring of tiny interlacing gold snakes.

Lord Rothlan raised his eyebrows as he and the MacArthur exchanged glances. They knew the significance of the ring even if Lewis didn't.

"It's a magic ring as well and," Casimir added dryly, "you won't ever lose it because I've hexed it to stay with you. I know how you leave things lying around all over the place."

"Will it grant me wishes, like you did?" Lewis asked.

Casimir smiled. "No, but it will protect you from harm and if you are ever in dire trouble, Lewis, I will come to your aid."

The sincerity in his voice brought tears to Lewis's eyes and Casimir smiled as he slipped the ring on his finger.

As the MacLeans crowded round to admire Lewis's ring, Casimir turned to look at Kitor. "I still have two presents to give," he announced gravely, "and the first one is for Kitor."

Kitor had been sitting very quietly on the Ranger's shoulder all evening, trying to avoid Casimir's glance. He knew the prince had noticed him and had asked about him for he'd seen him talking to Lord Rothlan and to Clara. They must have told him how he had lied to Prince Kalman to save Clara's life. He hoped that Casimir understood that he just couldn't have seen her killed by a thunderbolt.

The prince held his arm out. "Come, Kitor!" he commanded.

Everyone watched as Kitor flew to the prince. The poor bird was trembling as he flapped across the cave but one glance into the prince's eyes, reassured him.

"This, Kitor, is your present from me," Casimir said, gesturing towards the magic mirror.

Nothing happened for a few seconds and then the mirror rippled as a crow flew through it. Kitor's heart missed a beat. It couldn't be! Surely it couldn't be Cassia?

"Come, Cassia," the prince said, and she flew to him and perched beside Kitor.

Had everyone not started to clap, Kitor would most certainly have burst into tears. As it was, he fluttered his wings happily and the two birds sailed into the air and swooped round the cavern in delight at being together again.

There were tears in Clara's eyes, however, as she ran up to Casimir. "You couldn't have given Kitor a more wonderful present, Prince Casimir!" she said, wiping her eyes. "He's so happy!"

Kabad's name was called next and as the little water goblin moved shyly forward, Prince Casimir smiled gently and presented him with a small, slim spear. Kabad's eyes shone as he stammered his thanks. Everyone clapped as he hefted it in his hand; the balance was perfect and the steel tip shone, gleaming and sharp. Tears shone in his eyes as he bowed low to the prince. It was all that he needed to make life ideal for there were fish in his loch and now he could go hunting.

As Neil and Clara fussed round the little water goblin, admiring his spear, Lewis drew Prince Casimir to one side. "I'm glad that I went to Al Antara that night," he said, quietly. "I can't believe it only happened a few months ago — Jack, Colin and Peter seem like silly kids now and yet I was always so anxious to impress them! They must have thought me a real moron!"

"They're still young, Lewis. But like you, they'll be more sensible when they're older. You'll be fine now and you'll enjoy your new school, I'm sure."

Lewis suddenly burst out laughing. "You'll never believe it, Casimir, but I came out top in their entrance exam and the Headmaster said he'd never known a boy of my age with such an excellent knowledge of Scottish history! Mum and Dad were over the moon!" He paused. "And so was I," he said honestly. "I'd never have done it if I'd stuck to comics!"

"So all the reading we did in the Robinson's library was of use after all, then?"

"Yes, but it *was* interesting, Casimir. You know, when I grow up, I think I'd like to have a library like the Robinsons."

Casimir looked into the future and he smiled at Lewis. "You will, Lewis," he said. "You will."

34. Wheel of Fortune

As Murdo made his way up the High Street to Wullie's wee flat, he didn't appreciate the beauty of the scene around him. In fact he barely noticed it. It was snowing hard, the drifts were deep and the High Street, almost mediaeval in appearance, loomed vaguely through the driving flakes. His problems, however, were closer to home. His shoes were thin, he couldn't afford boots and his feet were already wet and freezing cold. Tammy Souter, who plodded along at his side, was cold as well. He drew his thin coat tighter round him and coughed continuously as he walked up the steep snow-covered street to Wullie's Close.

"Cheer up, Murdo," he said, grabbing him as he slipped on the icy pavement, "just be glad that we're here and not in a cell in Saughton Prison!"

Murdo nodded. There was always that. They were free men.

"I still can't work it out," Tammy said as they turned into Wullie's Close and started to climb the stairs. "They caught us fair and square!"

"Aye, but I did help Sir Archie, you know," Murdo said, thinking back to his interview with the Chief Constable. "I gave him the map of the Underground City, didn't I? And I was thinking, too, you know, that if he'd made a case against us then all the business of the ghosts would have had to come out into the open and I'm pretty sure he didn't want *that* to happen. I'm just glad that they didn't nick Wullie! He's not tough like us."

"Have you heard that he's given up smoking?" Tammy asked, grinning.

"Given up smoking? You must be joking! Wullie's a sixty a day man!"

"Auld Mrs Ramsay at the sweetie shop told me. Said her takings had gone down since he stopped!"

"I heard she was going to close down altogether," Murdo said, knocking on Wullie's door.

"Aye! Her man's ill and she can't run the wee shop all on her own."

They knocked on Wullie's door and waited expectantly as they heard the key turn in the lock. "Merry Christmas, Wullie," they said, pressing small gifts into his hands, "Merry Christmas!"

"Come away in," Wullie said, taking their coats. "Are your feet wet? Look, just put on these slippers."

Murdo understood the reason for the slippers when Wullie showed him proudly into his brand new living-room.

They stood gaping in complete and utter surprise at the transformation, for Wullie's living-room had, in the past, been a bit of a black hole. And that, I might add, is being charitable. Now it shone in shades of cream and warm reds. A big plasma TV set stood in one corner and a Christmas tree that reached the ceiling, decorated the other. Christmas decorations hung everywhere and the room was blissfully warm.

"Do you like it?" asked Wullie anxiously. "I've

stopped smoking, you see," he said proudly, "and I really had to have the whole place done over. It's a funny thing but ever since I met the ghosts in the Underground City I haven't been able to abide the smell of cigarette smoke. Makes me fair sick, it does!"

"But where did you get the money for all this?" demanded Murdo. "It looks as though you've spent a fortune!"

"Ocht," said Wullie reddening, "the wee woman in the shop was a decent body and she said I could take it all on credit and I don't have to pay anything back until next year!"

Murdo groaned. So Wullie had been conned into buying it all! "Why didn't you ask me first, you great idiot?" he said, appalled. "They've done you! She gets a whacking commission and you've probably sold your soul to a finance company for life. Do you know the interest they charge?"

Wullie shook his head, high finance not being his strong point. "No," he said, "they didn't mention that!"

"I bet they didn't!" growled Murdo. "Well, I'll go and see what I can do for you although it's probably too late!"

"Would you like some mulled wine?" Wullie asked, looking at them anxiously.

"Mulled wine?" Tammy Souter said, totally flabbergasted.

"Mulled wine!" Murdo repeated, in much the same tone.

"I was in Sainsbury's, you see," Wullie admitted, "and it was on offer!"

"Sainsbury's!" Murdo's mind went into over-drive. Wullie in Sainsbury's when he'd never been beyond the corner shop in his life!

"Well, we've been through a bad time what with the robbery going wrong and everything and I thought that … well, it's Christmas, isn't it! I wanted you to enjoy it. I've got the wine all ready, you know. It's heating up!"

Murdo and Tammy exchanged looks. It wasn't the dram they'd expected but they didn't want to spoil things for Wullie so, forcing a smile, they agreed that mulled wine was just the sort of thing to drink on Christmas Day.

The warmth of the room was having its effect and as they relaxed and looked round, they realized that Wullie really had gone to town in the furniture shop; pictures on the wall, ornaments and everything.

"Here we are," Wullie said, bringing the wine in on a tray. It was steaming and fragrant in posh glasses with silver holders. New as well, thought Murdo, worriedly. What else had the old biddy in the shop managed to sell him?

Two or three glasses of wine later, Murdo was not quite as observant but he still noticed that the generous slices of turkey, the crisp roast potatoes and delicious greens were not of Murdo's making. The mystery of his new cookery skills, however, was soon solved. Wullie beamed as he watched them eating the turkey hungrily. "Just tell me if you want another help-ing," he said casually. "It's no problem! The packets come frozen and I just have to pop them into my new microwave for a few minutes and they're ready."

It wasn't until they'd had second helpings of turkey and Christmas pudding that they sat back in their chairs and voted it the best meal they'd ever had. It was then that their eyes strayed to the presents, wrapped carefully in bright Christmas paper and decorated with big bows of red ribbon, lying under the Christmas tree. Neither Murdo nor Tammy had thought it good manners to mention them although they were sure that Wullie would have a couple there for them.

Wullie opened his gifts first. Murdo had given him a pair of gloves and Tammy had bought him a scarf. Wullie beamed at them. "Just what I needed," he confessed, delightedly. "The weather's been that bad lately."

Murdo and Tammy Souter sat up expectantly as he staggered over with a box from under the tree. "There are two for you, Murdo," he said, his face slightly red with exertion, "and these two," he said, hauling them over the carpet towards Tammy, "are yours!"

He watched them tear the paper. "I hope you don't mind," he said, smiling broadly, "but I've given you both the same thing."

It couldn't be chocolates, Murdo thought, ruling out that option immediately; chocolates didn't come in such huge boxes. What on earth could be inside them?

Then the banknotes spilled out onto the brand new red carpet. Hundreds of them! Thousands of them! Tammy tore the wrappers off the second present and there were more.

Wullie sat back in his chair and watched them with a huge grin on his face. This was his moment! He knew they thought him thick and most of the time he agreed with them. But this time he hadn't been thick! He'd been clever!

Murdo jumped to his feet, flinging banknotes in all directions. "Wullie! You great idiot! How did you do it?" he shouted.

Tammy sat, utterly thunderstruck, sifting the notes through his fingers. "They're all used and they're all fifties," he muttered, looking up at Wullie in awe. "There's a fortune here!"

The rest of the afternoon, needless to say, was spent counting the notes — lovingly, one by one.

"You see, I remembered what you told me, Murdo," Wullie explained, totally overcome by the praise they heaped on him. "I remembered you said that the folk in the pub would be suspicious if I walked through with a bin-liner full of cash so I stuffed all my clothes with as many banknotes as I could and just walked out. It was easy and not one of the coppers in the High Street stopped me on the way home or anything!" he said, beaming proudly.

"You carried all this money in your *coat?*" queried Murdo doubtfully, looking at the number of notes that littered the carpet.

Wullie looked at it, too, and frowned. "I must have done," he said, shaking his head. "When I emptied my pockets there … there just always seemed more to come. I wondered at the time …"

"It must have been magic," laughed Tammy Souter, not realizing how close he was to the truth. "Relax, Wullie, they're all genuine and they're all ours! What a Christmas this is!!"

"Wullie," Murdo said, sincerity ringing in his voice, "Wullie, you're a genius!"

"What are we going to do with it?" Tammy said. "What about a holiday in the south of France — or even Spain? Come on, lads, the three of us together!"

"That's a great idea," Murdo agreed, his eyes shining in his thin face.

Wullie, however, didn't seem so keen. "Well, you see," he said, "I've spent a lot of mine already on this furniture and stuff and I was thinking that with the rest of it I might buy Mrs Ramsay's wee shop."

"And sell sweeties?" Tammy said sharply. "Don't be a fool! She's been there for years and hasn't made a decent living out of it yet!"

"I wasn't thinking of selling sweeties," Wullie said, shaking his head. "I was thinking of starting one of these tourist shops that sell postcards and souvenirs and the like. They do a roaring trade all the year round and I've been making a bit selling them things, too."

"You've been *selling* them things? Nicked things, you mean?"

"No, Murdo, not nicked things. Things I made." He looked a bit embarrassed as he went over to the windowsill and picked up an ornament. "These," he said. "The tourists snap them up. Honest they do!"

Murdo held the pottery ornament in his hand. It was the Loch Ness monster and it was beautifully made. "When on earth did you start making these?" Murdo asked in surprise, turning it over in his hands.

"A while ago," Wullie confessed. "You know that I always carry a big lump of plasticine in my pocket in case I have to make impressions of keys in a hurry, don't you? Well, if I was ever bored I used to take it out and make models out of it. A chap in one of the shops told me I had a real knack for it and should go to Night School so that I could make things properly, out of clay. I didn't say anything to you, Murdo, 'cos I thought you'd laugh at the idea of me going to Night School but, well, I went and I had a great time and learned how to make things for the shops."

Murdo and Tammy looked at Wullie with real respect. It was only Murdo, however, who appreciated the effort it must have cost Wullie to approach the Night School on his own.

"You know, I think Wullie's right," Tammy Souter said slowly. "Running a shop's not a bad idea. We could all put in a share. It'll take a bit of cash to buy it and do it up — and then there'd be stock to buy, but I reckon it would be a going concern in no time."

"Wullie," they said, turning to a delighted Wullie, "you're a genius!"

35. Star Suspects

And, as it turned out, Wullie *was* a genius. From his original reproductions of the Loch Ness monster he swiftly progressed to bigger and better things. His spectacularly tall, fantastic castles are now collectors' pieces and his work is well-known throughout the length and breadth of Scotland.

Tammy and Murdo, it should be said, have settled to being respectable members of the community and although the shop's profits are split evenly three ways, they nevertheless make a good living out of it for it's always full of tourists who are enchanted at the wonderful selection of Scottish mementoes that fill the shelves.

If they are ever at the top of the High Street, Neil and Clara pop in to chat with Wullie who remembers them from the time they got lost in the Underground City. Being a good sort, he has never said a word to them about the ghosts because he thinks it might frighten them. It was on one of those occasions, when Neil and Clara were in his shop browsing for a present for their parents' anniversary, that they heard a familiar voice.

"Mr Lafferty," Clara said, looking up in delight. "How are you?"

"I hear that you've been a massive success in America," Neil said, shaking his hand. "A star!"

Matt Lafferty nodded. "It was really because of the pantomime," he said, "just one of those amazing things. Someone in the audience liked my style and I havena looked back since. Contracts just keep pouring in!" Neil and Clara looked at one another and smiled; the MacArthur, or more likely, the Sultan, had probably had a hand in it.

Lafferty's eyes sharpened and he lifted his eyebrows enquiringly as he caught sight of the ornament Clara had chosen for her parents — for there, on the counter, sat a beautifully crafted Loch Ness Monster.

"Oh, aye," he said, "what have we here, then?"

There was a silence as they looked at one another.

"It's a present for our parents," Neil explained uncomfortably.

"It's their anniversary," Clara added.

"It brings back memories, doesn't it? I'll maybe buy one for myself," Lafferty mused, picking it up and turning it over in his hand. "Mind you," he said, looking at them blandly, "it's missing something, isn't it?"

"Is it?" Clara asked nervously, her cheeks red.

"Well, it doesn't have a wee bit scarf hanging from its mouth, does it?"

Clara's face was a dead giveaway. She blushed again.

"You know, I'd fine like to meet that chap again — the ... er, you know, the fellow who played the ... *other* Sultan," Lafferty said, looking at them shrewdly. "He and I got on real well thegither. You'll be seeing him from time to time, will you?"

"Not that often, Mr Lafferty," Neil said, "but we'll ... we'll mention it to him when we do."

Wullie's face beamed as he wrapped Clara's parcel. Fancy Matt Lafferty being in his shop!! Just wait till he told Murdo and Tammy. They'd be gutted at missing him!

As Lafferty glanced speculatively round the shop, he found himself relaxing. It had a pleasant, comforting feel to it and idly scanning the multitude of souvenirs that crammed the shelves, his discerning eye quickly told him that it wasn't all tat. There were some quite artistic pieces among the tartan bits and bobs. He stiffened abruptly as he saw a dragon on one of the shelves, wings spread, horned head rearing fearsomely and just knew that he had to have it.

"I'll have this dragon as well," he said.

He placed it carefully on the counter as Clara took her parcel from Wullie. "It's a nice dragon," she said as Wullie lifted it and placed it carefully on another sheet of wrapping paper, "not at all fearsome really."

"And it's called Arthur," Neil added mischievously.

"Funny you should say that," Wullie said, staring at them in blank surprise. "I've always thought of it as Arthur. In my mind, it lives in Arthur's Seat and guards a heap of treasure."

Neil and Clara looked at one another.

"Perhaps it does," Neil said, his eyes sparkling as Matt Lafferty's eyebrows snapped together suspiciously.

"And we won't forget to mention your name to the Sultan when we next see him," Clara added seriously as they shook hands with him and waved goodbye.

"That was close," Neil muttered as the shop door closed behind them. "He suspects an awful lot!"

"What he said was true, though," Clara observed. "He and the Sultan did hit it off."

"Maybe we'll see him in the hill one day, then," mused Neil, "you never know."

"I'm glad for Wullie," Clara remarked as they wended their way down the length of the High Street. "His wee shop is lovely and he always seems to have lots of customers."

"I'm happy for him too," answered Neil, "but seeing him and Matt Lafferty together reminds me of Ali Baba and the Underground City. Life's a bit dull these days now that the pantomime's over."

"I shouldn't worry," Clara grinned as she waved to Mr MacGregor who was standing at the gates of their school. "Don't forget that Prince Casimir has invited us to spend half term at Ardray and we'll be staying with Lewis in Aberdeen at Easter."

"That's true!" Neil's eyes brightened considerable as he mentally totted up the weeks until half-term.

"I'm really looking forward to it," Clara mused dreamily. "With the MacArthurs around, life is never dull for long, is it? There always seems to be something happening in the world of magic."

As they walked down the Canongate, their eyes lifted involuntarily to the green slopes of Arthur's Seat that loomed behind the turreted grandeur of Holyrood Palace.

Clara smiled as she thought of Kabad — for the little goblin now lived in a very comfortable little home on Arthur's Seat. His eyes had shone with delight at his first view of Dunsapie Loch. High, quiet and secluded, with wonderful views over Edinburgh, it was an ideal spot.

"Think you'll like living here, then?" Neil had asked him.

Kabad's long fingers had gripped Clara's hand so tightly that she'd almost yelped. "Oh, yes!" came the delighted answer.

Archie, Jaikie and Hamish, who had taken an immediate liking to the little water goblin, explored the fringes of the loch with him, looking for a suitable cave or hole in the bank to give him shelter. It was a problem at first as the shoreline was quite open, but with their help, a rickety, disused jetty on the far side of the loch was cunningly converted to incorporate a concealed waterfront residence. Spacious, warm and comfortable, Kabad assures them that, by goblin standards, it is quite definitely palatial.

"We ought to visit Kabad tomorrow and see how he's getting on," Clara mused, stepping aside to avoid some tourists, clustered around the Scottish Parliament building. "It's a while since we've been upthere."

"Kabad?" said Neil. "Oh, he's doing all right. Kitor and Cassia visit the loch almost every day and according to them, he's still as happy as Larry! Spends his time fishing and playing with the ducks, apparently. He says he wouldn't go back to Loch Ness if you paid him."

Only a few people have spotted Kabad on the slopes of Arthur's Seat and then just for seconds.

He's happy and contented in his snug little home at the edge of the water, uses his beautiful, new spear to catch fish and finds the ducks, geese and seagulls much nicer company than the spiteful goblins of Nessie's caves.

In fact, if you are ever up there on a moonlit night, you might be lucky enough to spot him for he always dresses in his best clothes when visiting the MacArthurs — so if by any chance you're there and see a tiny figure walking by the loch, dressed in an ornate turban and a tunic and trousers of dark purple, shot with gleaming stripes of shiny, glittering gold … well, you'll know who he is, won't you? And you'll know where he's going …

Anne Forbes, *Dragonfire*

Clara and Neil have always known the MacArthurs, the little people who live under Arthur's Seat, in Holyrood Park, but they are not quite prepared for what else is living under the hill. Feuding faery lords, missing whisky, magic carpets, firestones and ancient spells ... where will it end? And how did it all start?

Set against the backdrop of the Edinburgh Fringe and Military Tattoo this is a fast-paced comic adventure, full of magic, mayhem and mystery ... and a dragon.

Contemporary Kelpies

Anne Forbes, *The Wings of Ruksh*

'For children who have read and enjoyed the Harry Potter series this is a fantastic title with which to continue their journey into the fantasy genre.'
— *Hilary Tomney, School Librarian Journal*

What lurks behind the magic mirrors? How are they connected to the missing Sultan's Crown and what secrets does the mysterious black tower hold?

From an Edinburgh literally cloaked in tartan, through the forbidding Highland hills, Neil and Clara set out on a perilous journey of winged horses and snow witches — and a reluctant broomstick.

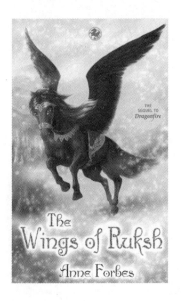

Contemporary Kelpies